"What's that terrible stink?" said Sharkadder. "Smells like dead skunk."

"It is," said Pongwiffy cheerfully. "It's tonight's supper. My specialty. You'll love it. Skunk stew. I'll just give it a stir," and she took a large ladle and poked at the heaving goo in the cauldron.

"Oh," said Sharkadder, wishing she'd stayed at home. "Skunk stew. Really?"

"I knew you'd be pleased," said Pongwiffy. "Now, tell me truthfully. How do you like the cave? It's a little damp, I know, and perhaps a bit small, but it was very cheap. Of course, it's a nuisance being in Goblin Territory, but I can't afford anything better at the moment. What do you think of it?"

"It's a dump," said Sharkadder. "It's a smelly little slum. It's not fit to live in. It's squalid and yucky. It's the worst cave I've ever been in. It suits you."

"It does, doesn't it?" agreed Pongwiffy, pleased. "I feel it's me. It's a pity about the Goblins, though. I'll tell you about them later. Now then. How much stew for you, Sharky?"

"Er—about half a teaspoon," said Sharkadder hastily . . .

Pongwiffy
by Kaye Umansky

Pongwiffy
Pongwiffy and the Goblins' Revenge
Pongwiffy and the Spell of the Year

KAYE UMANSKY

ILLUSTRATED BY CHRIS SMEDLEY

A MINSTREL® BOOK

Published by POCKET BOOKS
New York   London   Toronto   Sydney   Singapore

A Minstrel Book published by
POCKET BOOKS, a division of Simon & Schuster, Inc.
1230 Avenue of the Americas, New York, NY 10020

Text copyright © 1988 by Kaye Umansky
Illustrations copyright © 1988 by Chris Smedley

Originally published in Great Britain in 1988 by A & C Black, Ltd
Published by arrangement with A & C Black, Ltd

ISBN 978-1-4169-6832-0
ISBN 1-4169-6832-6

First Minstrel Books printing October 2001

10 9 8 7 6 5 4 3 2 1

A MINSTREL BOOK and colophon are registered trademarks of
Simon & Schuster, Inc.

For information regarding special discounts for bulk purchases,
please contact Simon & Schuster Special Sales at 1-800-456-6798
or business@simonandschuster.com

Front cover illustration by Sue Hellard

Printed in the U.S.A.

Contents

The Cast   vi

CHAPTER ONE
Entertaining   1

CHAPTER TWO
House Hunting   21

CHAPTER THREE
The Over-Familiar Familiar   39

CHAPTER FOUR
The Trial   58

CHAPTER FIVE
Little Pieces of Paper   78

CHAPTER SIX
Scott Sinister   92

CHAPTER SEVEN
The Contest   110

CHAPTER EIGHT
Preparations   130

CHAPTER NINE
Thieves   144

CHAPTER TEN
The Party   164

ALSO ⭐ The Goblins

STINKWART

PLUGUGLY · HOG · SLOPBUCKET · LARDO · EYESORE · SPROGGIT

AND (In order of appearance):

The Other Goblins

The Hedgehog Hair Rollers

Sharkadder's Broom

Pongwiffy's Broom

Sneering Wood Pigeons

Tree Demon With Knife

The Toad In The Hole

Scott Sinister

Lulu

Gnome with Umbrella And Fan

Butler/Coachman with Paper Bag Over Head (?)

Sunbathing She-Goblins

Talent Contest Audience: Skeletons, Banshees,
    Ghouls, Bogeymen, Werewolves, Trolls,
    Wizards in Disguise

The Witchway Rhythm Boys

Pierre De Gingerbeard

Dwarfs in Kitchen

Make-up/Hair By: Sharkadder

Costumes: Rags Incorporated

Music: Agglebag/Bagaggle, Macabre,
    Witchway Rhythm Boys

Produced By:
    Kaye *I owe it all to my husband* Umansky

Graphics: Chris *I did it for peanuts* Smedley

MISTY MOUNTAINS

CRAG HILL

SHARKADDER'S COTTAGE

PONGWIFFY'S HOVEL

TREE DEMON'S TREE HOUSE

WITCHWAY WOOD

WITCHWAY HALL

SOURMUDDLE'S COTTAGE

LOWER MISTY MOUNTAINS

GOBLIN HOME

GOBLIN TERRITORY

SCOTT SINISTER'S HOLIDAY RETREAT

GINGERBEARD'S KITCHENS (UNDERGROUND CAVERNS)

Scale: 1cm to 1 mile
0   1   2   3   4

N
W   E
S

CHAPTER ONE
ENTERTAINING

"Witch Sharkadder! My old friend!" cried Witch Pongwiffy, opening the front boulder with her very best welcoming smile firmly fixed in place.

"What a lovely surprise. Welcome to my humble cave. My, you do look nice. Is that a new hairdo, or have you had some sort of terrible shock, ha ha? Just my little joke. Come in, come in. Let me take your hat."

She seized the tall hat, gave it a respectful little brush and waited until Sharkadder's back was turned before booting it into a dark corner.

"It's hardly a surprise if you knew I was coming," remarked Sharkadder coldly, advancing into the cave. "I know you want to be my friend

1

again, Pongwiffy, but I'm not at all sure I want to be yours. Do stop putting it on."

There was no doubt that Pongwiffy was being revoltingly smarmy—but it was for good reason. You see, she and Sharkadder were usually best friends, but they had recently had one of their quarrels, and Pongwiffy was anxious to make amends.

"Oh, you're not still thinking about that silly old quarrel are you? Come on, Sharky, let bygones be bygones. Have a look at my new cave. I only moved in last week. You're my first guest."

Sharkadder stared around distastefully.

Pongwiffy's cave wasn't a pleasant sight. It had shocking damp problems for a start. Slimy green moss grew on the walls, and the floor was a seat of muddy puddles. The broken-down furniture wasn't so much arranged as thrown in any old how. Thick black steam belched from the horrible looking slop which bubbled and glopped in the cauldron.

"Well, sit down, Sharky, make yourself at home," fussed Pongwiffy, removing Sharkadder's cloak and dropping it into a slimy pool.

"There's nowhere to sit," observed Sharkadder truthfully.

"You'll have to use that cardboard box. I

haven't sorted the chairs out yet. That's the trouble when you've just moved in. It takes ages to get organized, doesn't it?"

"You've never been organized," said Sharkadder. "What's that terrible stink? Smells like dead skunk."

"It is," said Pongwiffy cheerfully. "It's tonight's supper. My specialty. You'll love it. Skunk stew. I'll just give it a stir," and she took a large ladle and poked at the heaving goo in the cauldron.

"Oh," said Sharkadder, wishing she'd stayed at home. "Skunk stew. Really?"

"I knew you'd be pleased," said Pongwiffy. "Now, tell me truthfully. How do you like the cave? It's a little damp, I know, and perhaps a bit small, but it was very cheap. Of course, it's a nuisance being in Goblin Territory, but I can't afford anything better at the moment. What do you think of it?"

"It's a dump," said Sharkadder. "It's a smelly little slum. It's not fit to live in. It's squalid and yucky. It's the worst cave I've ever been in. It suits you."

"It does, doesn't it?" agreed Pongwiffy, pleased. "I feel it's me. It's a pity about the Goblins, though. I'll tell you about them later. Now then. How much stew for you, Sharky?"

"Er—about half a teaspoon," said Sharkadder

hastily. "I had a huge lunch. And I think I've got a touch of tummy trouble. And I'm slimming."

"Nonsense," said Pongwiffy, relentlessly approaching with a huge, greasy plateful. "Get that down you. You don't need to slim. You're beautifully thin. You could model rags with that figure. And that's a lovely perfume you're wearing. Don't tell me—let me guess. Night In a Fish Factory, right? And I do *so* like the new hairstyle. It really suits you. Brings out the beakiness of your nose."

"It does, doesn't it?" agreed Sharkadder, finally coming around after such an onslaught of flattery. She scrabbled in her bag, took out a small, cracked hand mirror and examined the frazzled mess with satisfaction.

"I've got some new hair rollers," she explained. "Little hedgehogs. You warm them up. Not too much, or they get bad tempered and nip. Just enough to send them to sleep. Then you wind the hair around, and wait for them to cool. And it comes out all curly, like this."

"Beautiful," nodded Pongwiffy through a mouthful of stew. "You always look so nice, Sharky. I don't know how you do it."

"Yes, well I do try to take care of myself," agreed Sharkadder, tossing her tangles and applying sickly green lipstick. "You'd look a lot better yourself if you washed once in a while. And changed that disgusting old cardigan."

"What's wrong with my cardigan?" asked Pongwiffy, clutching the offending garment to her bony chest.

"What's right with it? It's got holes. It's got no buttons. You've spilled so many droppings down it, you can hardly see the pattern. It looks like it's been knitted with congealed egg. Want me to go on?"

"No," muttered Pongwiffy sulkily.

But it was true. Pongwiffy's sense of personal hygiene left a lot to be desired.

"As for those flies that buzz around you all day long, it's time you swatted them," added Sharkadder, enjoying herself.

"Swat Buzz and Dave? Never!" declared Pongwiffy, aghast at the idea. She was fond of her

flies. They circled around her hat, shared her food, and slept on her pillow at night.

"Look, let's not talk about flies and cardigans. You'll never change me, Sharky. I like the way I am. Try some stew. I made it specially."

"I can't. I haven't got a spoon," hedged Sharkadder.

"What on earth do you need a spoon for? Slurp it from the plate, like I'm doing," said Pongwiffy, demonstrating.

"No, I want a spoon," insisted Sharkadder.

Pongwiffy sighed and went to the sink. Sharkadder watched her crawl under the table, duck under the cobwebs, heave a heavy wardrobe to one side and kick a dozen cardboard boxes out of the way.

"I don't know how you bear it," said Sharkadder with a shudder. "Don't you ever tidy up?"

"Nope," said Pongwiffy truthfully, retracing her route with the spoon.

Sharkadder eyed it with a critical frown. "It's dirty," she observed. "What's all this crusty stuff?"

"Last week's skunk stew," explained Pongwiffy. "No point in washing it, seeing as we're having the same. Now, what was I going to tell you? Oh yes. My new neighbors. You see . . ."

"I want a clean spoon," interrupted Sharkadder.

The strain of being a polite hostess was suddenly more than Pongwiffy could bear.

"Honestly!" she shouted. "You're such a fusspot sometimes. I go to all the trouble of inviting you for supper, and all you do is . . ."

Just at that moment, there came an interruption. There was an ear-splitting crash, and the walls shook. The Goblins in the cave next door had arrived home. You should know quite a bit about the Goblins Next Door, because they feature rather a lot in this story.

The Goblins Next Door consisted of a whole Gaggle. A Gaggle? That's seven Goblins. These

were called Plugugly, Stinkwort, Eyesore, Slopbucket, Sproggit, Hog and Lardo. They moved in a week ago, about the same time as Pongwiffy, and they had already caused her no end of aggravation.

This seems a good time to tell you a little about Goblins in general. Then you can decide for yourself whether or not you would care to live next door to them.

The most important thing you should know about Goblins is this: they are very, very, *very* stupid. Take the business of their hunting night—Tuesdays. That's when they hunt. It's Traditional. Whatever the weather, every Tuesday they all troop out regardless and spend from dusk till midnight crashing about the woods hoping to catch something. They never do. It's common knowledge that the Goblins are out on Tuesdays, so everyone with any sense stays safely indoors and has an early night.

The Goblins are always surprised to find the woods deserted—but they'd never think of changing their hunting night to, say, Thursdays, thus catching everyone unawares. That's how stupid they are. Of course, you could forgive them their stupidity if they weren't so generally all around horrible.

After the futile hunt, Goblins always have a party. The party is always a flop, because there's never anything to eat, and invariably ends with a big fight. Goblins like fighting. It goes with their stupidity, and the Tuesday night punch-up has now developed into a Goblin Tradition. It's a silly one—but then, all their Traditions are silly. Here are a few more, just to give you the idea:

Painting Their Traps Bright Red; Bellowing Loud Hunting Songs While Walking on Tiptoe; Stomping Around in Broad Daylight with Faces Smeared with Soot so they won't be noticed; Wearing Bobbly Hats, even in a heat wave, To Stop The Brains Freezing Up; Cutting the Traditional Hole in the Bottom of the Hunting Bag, so that whatever goes in immediately falls out again. Right, that's enough about Goblins in general. Let's now get back to the Gaggle in the cave next door to Pongwiffy.

All Goblins are great music lovers, and Pongwiffy's new neighbors were no exception. They kept her up to all hours, playing ghastly Goblin music at very high volume. Now, Goblin music sounds rather like a combination of nails scraping on blackboards, burglar alarms, and dustbin lids blowing down the road, so you see what she had to put up with.

It was most unfortunate, then, that the Gaggle next door chose the very night that Pongwiffy was entertaining Sharkadder to supper to hold their Official Cave Warming Party.

Just take a look at the following:

7 Goblins make a Gaggle

3 Gaggles make a Brood

2 Broods make a Tribe

1 Tribe makes life unbearable.

The Gaggle next door had invited no less than *two entire Tribes* to their cave warming—and that, if you can't work it out for yourself, is eighty-four Goblins! They all arrived at the same time, singing. Can you imagine?

A hundred squabblin' Goblins,

Hobblin' in a line,

One got stuck in a bog, me boys,

Then there were ninety-nine . . .

they howled joyfully, pouring into the cave. Next door, Sharkadder leaped from her cardboard box, sending the plate of Skunk stew crashing to the floor.

"My new neighbors," explained Pongwiffy, scooping the spilled stew onto her own plate. "I'll eat this if you don't want it."

Ninety-nine squabblin' Goblins,

Hobblin' out to skate,

One went under the ice, me boys,

Then there were ninety-eight . . .

warbled the Goblins relentlessly, stomping around in their hobnail boots and beating their warty heads against the wall. A small avalanche of stones rained down on Sharkadder's new hairdo. A large spreading crack indicated that the ceiling was about to fall in.

"Stop them! Stop them making that dreadful noise!" howled Sharkadder, trying in vain to protect her curls.

Ninety-eight squabblin' Goblins,

Hobblin' down to Devon,

> *One got chased by a bull, me boys,*
>
> *Then there were ninety-seven . . .*

droned on the song, and Pongwiffy's favorite poison plant keeled over and died on the spot.

Then the ceiling *did* fall in. There was a groaning, grinding noise, and down it came with a huge crash, burying both Pongwiffy and Sharkadder under several tons of rubble. Luckily, they're Witches—and Witches are tough.

"Sharky? Where are you? Are you all right?" called Pongwiffy, crawling out from under a large slab of granite and peering through the murk at the fallen boulders littering the floor. There was a moment's silence. Then, the overturned cauldron gave a heave, and Sharkadder emerged, shaking with fury and covered from head to foot in Skunk stew.

"Oh dear," said Pongwiffy. "Sorry about that."

"I'm never speaking to you again, Pongwiffy!" hissed Sharkadder, and ran weeping from the cave.

> *Ninety-four squabblin' Goblins,*
>
> *Hobblin' out to tea . . .*

Pongwiffy picked her way through the rubble and staggered out, gasping for air. She was just in time to see Sharkadder mount her Broomstick, which was saddled outside, and zoom off, splattering the treetops with Skunk stew and screaming shocking curses. Pongwiffy's own Broom was propped where she had left it, fast asleep as usual.

One got choked by a crumb, me boys,

Then there were ninety-three . . .

Pongwiffy marched up to the Goblins' front door, which was, to be exact, their front boulder and rapped sharply.

There was a sudden pause, followed by muffled mutters of: "Fink dat's Uncle Slobbergum?" "No, he's already here." "Where?" "In de soup. He just fell in it." "See who it is, Stinkwart." "Where's Plugugly? Answering the boulder's his job . . ." and so on.

Finally the boulder rolled back, and Pongwiffy found herself staring into the repulsive, lumpy countenance of Plugugly, the biggest Goblin.

"Yer?" he growled, scratching unpleasantly and glaring at Pongwiffy with small, red, piggy eyes.

"How many more? How many more verses to that wretched song?" demanded Pongwiffy in a shrill voice.

"Derrrrrr . . ." Plugugly thought deeply, his brow creased in concentration. Maths wasn't his strong point.

"Wait dere," he said, and vanished to confer with the others inside. Pongwiffy tapped her foot impatiently while the whispered arguments went on, and grimly fingered the Wand which hung on a dirty string around her neck. Eventually Plugugly returned.

"Ninety-two," he said. "Yer."

"Over my dead body," Pongwiffy said.

"If you like," Plugugly said, leering.

"Do you realize," snapped Pongwiffy in her firmest, no-nonsense voice. "Do you realize that you have brought my ceiling down? You've quite ruined my supper party. You've upset my stew, not to mention my best friend. I haven't slept a wink for days—not since you moved in. Every night I have to listen to your caterwauling. There's a limit to my patience. Who d'you think you are anyway?"

"Goblins," said Plugugly with the confidence that comes from having the body of a bolster topped with a face like an old, squeezed tea bag.

"Goblins. Dat's what we is. And we does what we likes."

"Oh you do, do you? And suppose I put a spell on you, and *banish you from this cave*?" Pongwiffy produced this ace from her sleeve with an air of triumph.

"Derrrrrr . . . wait dere," ordered Plugugly, and retreated inside again. Pongwiffy waited. After a few moments, he returned.

"You better come in," he said. "Yer."

It was grim and gloomy in the Goblin cave. The air was thick with dense smoke curling from the torches jammed into crevices in the walls. There was an overpowering smell of Goblin, which threatened to overwhelm even Pongwiffy's own personal odor—and that's not easy, as you would know if you ever stood downwind of her. Holding her nose, she peered around.

One hundred and sixty-eight small, red, piggy eyes peered right back at her. Everywhere she

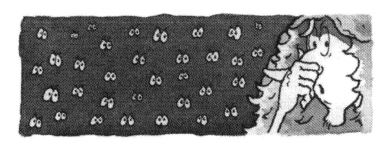

looked, there were Goblins. They sneered from the shadows, scoffed in the corners and gibbered and jeered in the gloom.

Some wore the Traditional Goblin Uniform, which is baggy trousers held up with braces, and, of course, the time-honored bobbly hat. Others wore stolen leather jackets dripping with chains and studs. These were members of an outlaw Goblin brood from a grotto high in the Misty Mountains. They called themselves the Grottys, and would dearly have liked to own motorbikes. So far, however, they only possessed one rusty tricycle between them which they took turns falling off.

There were lizardlike, scaly Goblins, grossly fat Goblins, hairy Goblins, bald Goblins, drooling Goblins, scraggy little weasly ones with long noses, tall spindly ones with short noses, and Goblins with humps, lumps, and bumps in the most surprising places. All of them wore huge boots, all had small red piggy eyes, and all looked and smelt as though they had crawled out of a blocked-up drain.

"Roight, boys!" said Plugugly. "Bit of 'ush if you *please.* Our neighbor wants a word. Yer."

The Goblins sniggered and nudged each other.

"Yes," said Pongwiffy severely. "I do. I'm getting very tired of you lot. In fact, I'm not putting up with another minute of it. You've brought my ceiling down. My best friend's not speaking to me and my hot water bottle's punctured. It's a disgrace. In fact, I'm seriously thinking of casting a Spell of Banishment on you. What do you say to that, eh?"

To her surprise, none of the Goblins looked the least bit worried. In fact, several of them tittered. One even *yawned.*

"So I'm warning you now," continued Pongwiffy uneasily. "Any more noise, and that's it. Whoosh, gone, the pack of you."

"Let's see yer do it," croaked Slopbucket, sidling closer.

"Her her her. Yer, let's see yer do it!" was the general cry.

"I will!" threatened Pongwiffy. "I will, too. Unless you promise to remove your boots and whisper from now on. Do you?"

"NO!" came the howled chorus. "NO! NO! NO!" And they cheered and began a slow hand clap as Pongwiffy seized her Wand and held it aloft.

Now, that was very odd, for a Witch's Wand is guaranteed to put fear into the heart of any Goblin. Brutes, bullies and thorough-going pests that they are, they have one disadvantage, apart from being stupid. They Can't Work Magic.

Pongwiffy gave her wand a little shake to make sure it was working. Green sparks crackled at the tip and it began to hum. All was well.

"Here I go! One Banishing Spell coming up!" And she began the chant.

> *Blow you winds with all your might,*
>
> *Blow these Goblins from my sight,*
>
> *Where you blow them I don't care,*
>
> *'Long as they're not here, but there!*

Nothing happened. The Goblins nudged each other, grinning. Pongwiffy frowned at her Wand and tried again.

Still nothing. Then she became aware of wheezing chortles and horrible strangled snorting noises. The *Goblins were laughing!*

They fell about, digging each other in the ribs and hooting with mirth.

"I don't understand it," mumbled Pongwiffy, staring aghast at her Wand, which had ceased to spark, or even hum, *and had a knot in it!* "It's always worked before . . ."

"It's quite simple, really," explained Plugugly, mopping his streaming eyes. "It's like this, yer see. *We bin banished already*! To this 'ere cave. So you're stuck wiv us. Har har har!"

"*What?*"

"True as I'm standin' 'ere, ain't it, boys? It were a Wizard what done it. At our lass place. 'E comes complainin' about the noise, see, just like you. We gives 'im a bit o' lip, see, an' in the end 'e declares us a—what were it again?"

"Public Nuisance!" roared the Goblins with great pride.

"Yer, dat's it. Public Nuisance. So 'e gives us the boot 'n banishes us 'ere. An' 'ere we gorra stay. Fer ever. *So your feeble ole spells won't work!*" Which was true. Wizard Magic is strong stuff, and not easily undone.

"Her her her," wheezed Plugugly, shoulders heaving. "Worra laugh ain't it, eh?"

"No," snapped Pongwiffy coldly. "It isn't."

"Tell yer what, though," continued Plugugly. "We can come to a—wassit called again?"

"Compromise?" said Pongwiffy hopefully.

"Yer, dassit. Compromise. You don't come around 'ere again complainin', and we won't smash yer place up. 'Ows that sound? Reesnubbo?"

It didn't sound reasonable at all. Pongwiffy glared into his grinning, stupid face and debated whether to punch him on the nose or move out the next day.

She moved out the next day.

CHAPTER TWO

HOUSE HUNTING

"It's very kind of you to put me up, Sharky," said Pongwiffy to Sharkadder one week later. They were in the kitchen of Sharkadder's small cottage in Witchway Wood at the time.

"That's all right, Pong," lied Sharkadder with fingers crossed behind her back. She had, of course, forgiven Pongwiffy for the disastrous supper party. After all, it hadn't been her fault, as Sharkadder had to admit when Pongwiffy had groveled long enough.

However, there was a limit to friendship. Pongwiffy had been sleeping in Sharkadder's spare room for over a week now, and was showing no signs of moving out. Sharkadder was a house-proud Witch, as Witches go, and Pongwiffy was a Witch of Dirty Habits.

They were sitting at the breakfast table. Sharkadder, who was slimming, had made do with a glass of fresh newt juice. Pongwiffy, who wasn't, had worked her way through two plates of lice crispies, three griffin eggs, a pile of toast with jelly-fish jam and thirteen cups of hot bogwater. She had also finished the trifle from the night before.

21

"I suppose I'll have to start looking for a place of my own one day," said Pongwiffy, licking the trifle plate clean.

"Oh, really? What a pity," said Sharkadder insincerely. "I'll just go and get the paper, then. We'll see if there's anything suitable." And without even bothering to put on her lipstick, she ran out the door with what Pongwiffy considered to be indecent haste.

Pongwiffy finished up Sharkadder's newt juice and went to the cupboard to raid the biscuit tin, keeping a close eye on Dead Eye Dudley. Dudley was Sharkadder's Familiar—a huge, battered black tomcat with one yellow eye, a crooked tail and a very, *very* bad temper.

Rumor had it that Dudley spent one of his nine lives as ship's cat on a pirate ship. This would account for the eyepatch he wore, and his habit of growling strange, piratical sayings. Everybody was terrified of Dudley, except Sharkadder who loved him dearly. Right now he was asleep on the hearth rug, claws flexing as he dreamed of chasing rats in the hold and wailing sea chanties under a tropical moon.

Pongwiffy hastily crammed the last three mustard creams into her mouth and wondered whether Sharkadder would notice if she cut herself a piece of that delicious looking fungus sponge hidden on the top shelf. Before she could decide, she heard Sharkadder's footsteps hurrying down the path. Hastily she scuttled back to the table and repositioned herself, humming a casual little hum.

In came Sharkadder with the *Daily Miracle* under her arm. She glanced disapprovingly at the pool of spilled bogwater, crumbs, broken eggshells and other assorted droppings at Pongwiffy's feet, and signaled to her Broom. It leaped to attention and briskly proceeded to sweep the mess under the rug, giving Pongwiffy's ankles several sharp raps in the process.

Pongwiffy's own Broom came hurrying up to join in. This cleaning business was quite a novelty. Normally, it never did a thing between flights except sleep. Pongwiffy briskly kicked it back into the corner. If there was one thing that annoyed her, it was a domesticated Broom.

Sharkadder tutted and opened the windows to let in some fresh air. Fond as she was of her friend, there was no denying that Pongwiffy's odor tended to get a bit overpowering at times. She cleared a space in the breakfast debris and spread out the newspaper, running a finger down the *FOR SALE* column.

"Now then, let's see. Here's one: *Igloo. North Pole. Apply Yeti, Greenland.*"

"Too far," said Pongwiffy firmly. "Too cold."

"Hm. All right, what about this? *Pretty little cottage with roses around door. All clean and spanky shiny. Lovely views.*"

"Yuck. Sounds awful," shuddered Pongwiffy.

"Here's another one, then: *Cave. Goblin territory. No ceiling. Otherwise perfect.*"

"That's where I've just come from! No thanks."

"Well, that's all there is today. Oh, wait a minute, this sounds interesting. Listen: *Tree house for sale. Own landing platform. Ideal for high flying witches. Every mod. con.*"

"What's that mean?"

"Really, don't you know anything? Modern Contraptions, of course," said Sharkadder, who was a bit of a know-all at times. "It sounds ideal," she continued. "We'll go and take a look right away."

"What—now?" bleated Pongwiffy, eyeing the toaster sadly.

"Certainly. We must strike while the iron is hot," replied Sharkadder, and bustled away to put on her lipstick.

By the time Pongwiffy had exchanged her filthy old dressing gown for her filthy old cardigan and chased the spiders from her hat, the iron had cooled considerably—but they went anyway.

"I don't like it," muttered Pongwiffy, eyeing the distant tree house doubtfully.

It looked very high up indeed, and Pongwiffy is one of those Witches who can only stand heights if there's a Broomstick clamped firmly between her knees.

"Nonsense. You can't even see it from down here," said Sharkadder.

"That's what I mean. It's too high. I wish I had my Broom." Pongwiffy hadn't been able to persuade her Broom to come. It had become friendly with Sharkadder's, and wanted to stay behind and help sweep up. When Pongwiffy argued, it merely swept away and returned with a copy of the Coven Rule Book, pointing a bristle at the rule which said, "Daytime flying on Broomsticks is strictly forbidden."

"Well, you haven't, and that's that," snapped Sharkadder. She was beginning to suspect that Pongwiffy had no intention of leaving—ever. Which was true. Pongwiffy enjoyed the breakfasts too much. "You'll just have to climb the rope ladder, same as anyone else," she added.

"Can I borrow your Wand?" asked Pongwiffy hopefully. Hers was still in a state of trauma after trying, unsuccessfully, to cancel out Wizard Magic.

"Certainly not!" Sharkadder was shocked at the request. Wands are not to be used lightly. Serious Magic is what they are intended for, and planting lazy Witches in treetops could not be considered as Serious. Besides, they weren't supposed to borrow Wands. It was against The Rules, like daytime flying of Broomsticks.

"You go first, then," said Pongwiffy.

"No," said Sharkadder, who didn't like the look of the rope ladder either. "No, I'll spoil my makeup. I'll stay down here and catch you if you fall."

"Thanks very much," Pongwiffy snapped, nastily.

"Not at all," snapped back Sharkadder, even more nastily, and made a note to break friends as soon as Pongwiffy was settled.

Swallowing hard, Pongwiffy caught hold of the flimsy ladder, and set her foot on the bottom rung. It swayed alarmingly.

"What's the matter? Scared?" jeered Sharkadder, seeing her hesitate.

"Who, me? Certainly not," said Pongwiffy, and started up the lower rungs at a bold run.

She had only scrambled some ten feet when she began to slow down. She already sensed that she was unnaturally high. The air felt colder already. A chilly gust of wind blew up her cardigan, and she gripped the thin ropes more firmly.

"How much farther?" she called down, not liking to look up.

"Lots," came Sharkadder's voice from below.

She sounded shockingly far away. "Keep going, you've hardly started!"

Pongwiffy gulped and forced herself to move on up. Her knees scraped on the tree trunk as she climbed, bits of moss and tree bark fell in her eyes and her cardigan kept getting hooked up on the smaller branches.

A fat wood pigeon flew past her head, staring in puzzlement before flying away. Pongwiffy risked a glance up. The tree house seemed even farther away now than it did from the ground.

"Hurry up!" called Sharkadder. "I can't wait all day, I've got important things to do!"

Her voice rang with a worrying new echo. Pongwiffy looked down, and trembled at what she saw.

Sharkadder had turned into a midget. From this angle, her body had disappeared, and only her small, upturned white face with the slash of green lipstick could be seen.

Pongwiffy's hat fell off, and she stifled a squawk as she watched it drop dizzyingly through space. Her arms ached, her stomach

churned, and she felt sure she was catching a cold. The wind blew stronger, and a hoarse cooing filled the air. The wood pigeon had returned with a gang of friends in order to watch her ordeal.

They settled on the outlying branches of the tree and watched with keen interest as Pongwiffy hoisted herself still higher.

"Mustn't look down. Mustn't look down," Pongwiffy mumbled through dry lips as the wind dragged at her rags. The tree, which looked so stout from the ground, suddenly felt very unstable, as though it might topple over at any minute.

"Yoo-hoo! Pong!" Sharkadder's voice floated up. It might be important. Perhaps she was trying to warn Pongwiffy of some hazard she hadn't yet seen. Unwillingly, Pongwiffy looked down.

"I've got your hat, Pong! It's quite safe!" called Sharkadder, waving it merrily. Pongwiffy nearly wept.

"You're nearly there now. Keep going!"

Pongwiffy was now so high that it was hard to

make out Sharkadder's words. Sniveling, she dragged herself up a few more rungs while the posse of wood pigeons sniggered unsympathetically. One of them took off, hovered just above her head and dropped something rather unkind on her shoulder. The rest thought that was hysterically funny. The only one who wasn't laughing was Pongwiffy.

All too aware that she was running out of steam, she looked up. To her relief, Sharkadder was right. She had nearly gained the top rung. The sturdy tree house platform was only another few feet away. Desperately, she clawed at the ropes. One step . . . two steps . . . three . . . nearly there . . . almost . . . another rung . . .

"BOO!" said a voice. Inches away was the grinning face of a small green Tree Demon. It was

crouched on all fours, looking down over the platform edge. In its hand was a sharp knife. Pongwiffy very, *very* nearly let go with the shock—but not quite.

"What d'you want, Witch?" hissed the Tree Demon, waving the knife.

"A rest," said Pongwiffy.

"Not a chance. Not in my house. I don't like Witches."

"What do you mean, *your* house? This isn't *your* house. It's for sale."

"Not anymore it ain't. Bought it this morning. Paid a deposit. Early Tree Demon gets the worm, eh? Now, if you'd just move your hand a bit . . ."

And so saying, the Tree Demon took its sharp knife and cut through the rope ladder.

There was silence over the breakfast table the following morning. Sharkadder was daintily sipping her newt juice and picking at a plateful of scrambled ant eggs. Pongwiffy had her right arm in a sling and was staring gloomily at the stale crust which had been set before her. The standard of breakfast was definitely declining.

There was no doubt about it—she had outstayed her welcome. Sullenness hung in the air like a cloud. Dead Eye Dudley was sitting with his back to everybody, and even the Brooms were sulking. Pongwiffy had lectured hers at great length about its refusal to leave the house the previous day, never mind The Rules—who was the boss around here anyway—and Sharkadder's had come out in sympathy. At length, Pongwiffy broke the silence. Somebody had to.

"Are we going to look at any more houses today, then?"

Sharkadder shrugged. "You are. I'm not. *Hours* we wasted at the Witch doctor's yesterday. All for a little bruise on your elbow. You made me late back for Dudley's tea."

"Oh dear! Did I? Did I *really*? What about you, then? You almost had me killed! Call yourself a friend."

"What are you complaining about? I saved you, didn't I?"

"Yes, when I was about two inches from the ground!"

"I keep telling you, I only remembered the spell at the last minute. Wish I hadn't remembered it at all now. Here." Sharkadder threw the *Daily Miracle* at Pongwiffy. "Look for yourself. I'm tired of doing all the work."

Pongwiffy, without looking, declared that she

didn't like the sound of any of them. Sharkadder pointed out that beggars couldn't be choosers. Pongwiffy said that her arm still hurt and she couldn't be bothered. Sharkadder remarked that she had better be bothered.

"Because," she said spitefully. "Because you're not staying with me any longer."

Pongwiffy scowled. Things were heading for a crisis. She picked at her piece of dry bread and hummed mournfully to herself. Sharkadder finished her breakfast in silence, cleared away, painted her face, put on her hat and went out shopping. When she came back, Pongwiffy was slumped in the same position, looking forlorn and pulling threads from her sling.

Sharkadder cooked lunch and ate the lot in full view of Pongwiffy, who looked even sadder. Finally, Sharkadder could bear it no longer.

"All right!" she screamed. "All right! I'll come with you, just this once! Anything to get rid of you. But I claim the right to break friends first thing tomorrow morning. And that's when you go, Pongwiffy, whether you've found a house or not. Agreed?"

"Agreed," said Pongwiffy sniffily. "Never liked you much anyway."

• • •

What an awful day they had. They tried every single place that the *Daily Miracle* had to offer. They saw warrens, lairs and holes in the ground. They trailed through caverns, caves and cowsheds. They inspected a log cabin, a caravan and even a wigwam. They trooped tiredly around sheds, shacks and shantys. None of them, for one reason or another, was quite right. In desperation, Pongwiffy even agreed to look over the pretty little cottage with the lovely views. It was every bit as charming as the advertisement said it was. Pongwiffy loathed it.

The moon was beginning to rise as they wended their way to Sharkadder's place. They were quarreling loudly.

"I've never known such a fusspot," Sharkadder yelled.

"Well, I'm sorry, but I didn't like any of them," Pongwiffy yelled back.

"Well, just don't blame me when you're homeless tomorrow."

"Certainly I shall blame you. How you could throw out a homeless friend with a bad arm I just don't know."

"I'm not throwing a friend out. I'm throwing *you* out."

"I thought we weren't breaking friends till tomorrow," muttered Pongwiffy.

"That's when I'm throwing you out!"

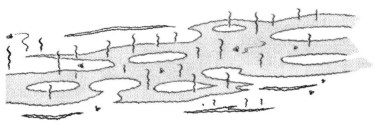

"How you could throw out a homeless friend with a bad arm I just don't know . . ."

And so on.

Suddenly, Pongwiffy stopped and sniffed. Sharkadder went marching on in a very bad temper indeed.

"Just a minute, Sharky," hissed Pongwiffy,

nose twitching. "That smell! That beautiful smell. What is it?"

"Smells like a rubbish dump," answered Sharkadder, trying not to breathe too deeply.

"That's it! That's exactly what it is! I was brought up on one of those, you know. Oooh, that smell . . . reminds me of my childhood. Do you think we could take a little look?"

"What, NOW?"

"Please, Sharky. It would mean so much to me. Ah, please."

"Oh——bother! Come *on* then, if you must," begrudged Sharkadder.

Together they followed their noses to the source of the smell. It wasn't far away.

"What a sight!" whispered Pongwiffy, awestruck. "A rubbish dump under the moon. Brings tears to the eyes."

"Hmm. Very nice." Sharkadder was fidgeting, wanting to get back home to Dudley.

"What's that over there?" Pongwiffy pointed. "There, look. No, *there*, idiot. Behind that pile of old mattresses. Left of the broken pram. Near the rusty cooker. Surely you can see. Look, over by the cat food tins. Right of that old carpet! There, see it? *There!*"

Sharkadder squinted. "What, that? You mean that broken-down old hovel?"

But Pongwiffy was off, running like the wind, as fast as her bent old legs would carry her. When Sharkadder caught her up, she was standing in the doorway of the broken-down old hovel.

The door was open—or, to be exact, it was lying among the weeds in a sea of flaking paint, having finally parted company with its rusty hinges. Broken windows sagged in their frames, and the roof was full of holes. A dreadful smell of damp and decay wafted from the dark interior. Pongwiffy was inhaling the stench, eyes closed in ecstacy.

"What *are* you playing at, Pong?" snapped Sharkadder crossly. "What's so special about an empty, smelly old hovel?"

Pongwiffy's eyes opened and she smiled and blinked as though coming around from a trance.

"Sharky," she said, with a happy grin. "Sharky, my old friend. This is it. The end of the line. I've found it. Welcome to my new home."

CHAPTER THREE

THE OVER-FAMILIAR
FAMILIAR

"Well? How are you settling in?" asked Shark-adder a few days later. Pongwiffy had popped in to borrow Sharkadder's spare cauldron. Her own, of course, was dented beyond repair. She was hanging around in the hope that Sharkadder might offer some breakfast.

"Wonderfully," said Pongwiffy. "I've nearly finished. I managed to rescue lots of stuff from the cave. It's lucky my Wand's better. I'd never have been able to lift all those boulders by myself. Of course, I didn't bother with some of it. It helps being next to the rubbish dump. I found all my furniture there, you know."

Strangely enough, although she tried to speak cheerfully, she sounded a bit glum.

"I hope you've cleaned it up a bit," remarked Sharkadder, who was sitting at a cracked mirror, gently warming her set of hedgehog hair rollers over a candle. Lipsticks and little bottles of nail varnish in hideous shades littered the table.

"Clean it? Whatever for? It's just perfect the way it is," said Pongwiffy. "Why don't you come and see this afternoon?"

"Too busy," said Sharkadder. "Dudley and I are working on a new spell."

"Oh," said Pongwiffy, disappointed. "Oh. Another time, then." And she gave a little sigh.

"What's the matter, Pong?" asked Sharkadder, seeing her friend's crestfallen face. "I thought you loved your new hovel."

"Oh, I do, I do. It's just . . . well, to be honest, Sharky, I'm feeling a bit lonely. It's very quiet at the rubbish dump. I haven't seen a soul in the last three days."

"Hmm. You know what you need," said Sharkadder, diving after a cross, overheated hedgehog who had plopped from the table and was desperately making for the door. "You need a Familiar. You're the only Witch I know who hasn't got one."

"I've got my flies," said Pongwiffy, pointing. Buzz and Dave came zooming back from the biscuit tin and circled loyally around the point of her tall hat.

"Flies? Flies don't count."

Buzz and Dave buzzed angrily. But she was right. Flies don't count. A Familiar, according to the dictionary is, "A demon attending and obeying a Witch." Familiars, however, don't have to be demons. They can be cats, owls, crows, bats—anything you like, really, as long as they've got a bit of intelligence. That puts the likes of Buzz and Dave right out of the running. There's so much to pack into a fly's small body, there's just no room for intelligence.

"Apart from anything else, think of the time you'd save," continued Sharkadder. "Don't you get tired of running your own messages and collecting your own ingredients? Not to mention doing all your own spying."

Pongwiffy had to confess that she did.

"There you are then! Stuck in that old hovel with only your Broom for company. No wonder you're fed up. You definitely need a Familiar. All the best Witches have them. I don't know what I'd do without darling Dudley. Put the kettle on, and we'll write an advertisement over a nice cup of hot bogwater. You can put it in the *Daily Miracle*."

Pongwiffy filled the kettle carefully. Shark-adder's darling was perched on the draining board next to the sink, crooning a sea chanty while sharpening his teeth with a file.

We pushed him off the plank, miaw,

We clapped him when he sank, miaw,

Oh what a jolly prank, miaw

When Filthy Frank was drowned-O!

sang Dudley in a low growl.

"What a pretty tune, Dudley," said Shark-adder. "I do love it when you sing."

Pongwiffy accidentally sprinkled three drops of water on the tip of Dudley's tail. Only three little drops, that's all, but you should have heard him!

"Ye cack-handed, clumsy old crow, I'll hang ye from the yardarm! I'll have ye pulverized and thrown to the fishes, be danged if I don't!"

"He likes you really," said Sharkadder, rolling up the last hedgehog. "That's just his way of speaking." She took a bottle marked *Old Sock* and dabbed some behind her ears. "Want some?"

"No," said Pongwiffy proudly. "I have my own

built-in smell." True. Compared to Pongwiffy, *Old Sock* smells like a garden of roses.

"Now, we need a paper and pencil, then we must put on our Thinking Caps." Sharkadder bustled about in a businesslike way.

"I haven't brought mine," said Pongwiffy.

"Never mind, we'll take turns with mine. Come to Mother, Dudley, and sit on my lap."

Dudley stretched, yawned and thumped heavily onto Sharkadder's bony knees. He rubbed himself against her chin, purring loudly.

"Isn't he sweet? Isn't he a darling? He's my Dudley. My cuddly-wuddly Dudley," cooed Sharkadder adoringly, picking hairs off her lipstick. "Of course, you'll never find a Familiar like Dudley, Pong. Not many Witches are so lucky."

"No," agreed Pongwiffy, hoping that her bad luck would hold. She certainly didn't want a familiar like Dudley.

All that day they worked on the advertisement. The floor was a sea of screwed-up pieces of paper and broken pencils before they got it just right. Even the Thinking Cap was fit for nothing, and had to be thrown away.

"It's rather good, isn't it?" said Pongwiffy

many hours later, peering with red, bleary eyes at the finished product.

"It's brilliant," agreed Sharkadder, who had done most of the work. "Read it again. I could listen to it all night."

WANTED FAMILIAr , APPLY to
Witch Pongwiffy, The Hovel,
Dump Edge , witchway Wood,
No time wasters .

Sharkadder stood up and began taking the hedgehogs from her hair. She placed them tidily in a little box, where they lay in rows, still snoring.

"I'm sure that'll do the trick, Pong. Good job you had me to help you."

"It was," said Pongwiffy gratefully. "Thanks, Sharky. Thanks for the meals too. You're a good friend." And off she went to post it.

By the following night, Pongwiffy had forgotten all about her advertisement. She was too busy preparing her supper to think about anything else. Her supper was giving her problems. It was Toad-in-the-Hole. She had made the Hole—a nice deep one in the lumpy gray batter. The trouble lay in getting the Toad to stay in it. Every time she turned her back to reach for the salt, out its head would pop again, a tetchy expression on its face.

"I've told you a hundred times. Get back down and *stay* down," snapped Pongwiffy, puffing up the fire with the bellows.

"Why?" complained the Toad, who liked explanations.

"Because you're my supper, that's why! Now, get back in that Hole!"

"Shan't," sulked the Toad.

Pongwiffy whacked it smartly on the head with a spoon. The Toad submerged, muttering vague threats.

"Now then, what next? Ah yes. Lay the table."

Laying the table wasn't as easy as it sounds. Tottering towers of dirty dishes reached almost to the rafters. They had been growing steadily taller all week, for Pongwiffy, being a Witch of Dirty Habits, couldn't be bothered to clear them away. Her Wand was somewhere around. Probably on the table, buried under the groaning piles of dishes. Some had green mold on them, the ones at the top were festooned with cobwebs, and a family of cockroaches had set up house in one of the teacups.

"Oh well," said Pongwiffy with a frown. "Suppose I'll just have to clear these away."

She stretched out a finger, and gave the nearest tower a little push. It teetered for a moment, then toppled slowly, crashing to the floor in a nasty mess of broken china and moldy leftovers. Pongwiffy collapsed into the nearest chair, exhausted. She wasn't used to housework.

That was when the doorbell rang.

"Oh—botheration! Who's that?"

Hastily she glanced at her reflection in a bent teapot, and rubbed a bit of dirt into her nose. The doorbell continued to ring with an insistent, irritating, teeth-on-edge jangling.

"Answer it! Answer it!" begged the Toad, who

had a bad headache. Unable to bear the racket, it plunged back into the batter and tried to relax.

"All right, all right!" snarled Pongwiffy, hobbling to the door and snatching it open.

First, she thought there was no one there. Then, she saw it. A small, cute, honey-colored Hamster with pink paws was dangling by its teeth from her bell rope. As it swung from side to side, the cracked bell continued to jangle harshly inside the hovel.

"Here—hang on a minute! Get *down* from there!" ordered Pongwiffy severely.

"Vat I do?" asked the Hamster with difficulty, speaking between clenched teeth. " 'Ang on or get down?"

"Get *down!*"

The Hamster dropped down, light as a leaf, nose twitching.

"Coo. Vat a pong. You are Pongwiffy. Ya, I come to ze right place." And the Hamster scuttled past her into the hovel, leaving a trail of minute paw marks in the thick dust coating the floor.

What a cheek! Pongwiffy was speechless.

"Is big tip in 'ere," remarked the Hamster, staring around. "Don't you not never do no 'ousework?"

"Big *tip*? How dare you!" said Pongwiffy, finding her voice at last. "I don't know who you think you are, but I want you out of my hovel, this minute."

" 'Ugo," said the Hamster, still looking around.

"I *beg* your pardon? *Me* go?" Pongwiffy couldn't believe her ears.

"Nein, nein! Is name. 'Ugo. Viz an *H*."

"Well, look here, Hugo-with-an-*H*, I don't know what you want, but . . ."

"I vant ze job."

"Job? What job?"

"Vitch Familiar. I see advert in paper. I come for interview. So. Interview me."

And Hugo-with-an-*H* climbed up the table leg and settled himself comfortably against the bent teapot, paws folded in his lap.

"I shall do no such thing. You're not suitable. Goodbye."

" 'Ow you know zat till you interview me?" asked Hugo reasonably.

"I can tell. We Witches know these things. You're just not the right type. Traditionally speaking."

"Vat is right type?" Hugo had found a pile of crumbs, and was busily stuffing them into his cheek pouches.

"Well—cats, of course. Weasels, ferrets, stoats, that sort of thing. Bats. Crows. Toads occasionally, if you can find an intelligent one." Pongwiffy glared spitefully at the Toad-in-the-Hole, who had its head stuck out as usual and was listening with interest to the conversation.

"The thing is," she continued. "The *main* thing is, a good Familiar has to be ugly or wicked, or better still, both. A good Familiar is *never* cute and fluffy. With a silly accent."

"Meanink me?" enquired Hugo. He spoke mildly, but there was a dangerous glint in his eye.

"Most certainly. Just look at yourself. You're sweet and cuddly. To a disgusting degree, actually. But then, you're a Hamster. You lot are supposed to be cute. Nice, gentle little things who live in cages and get tickled under the chin, like this . . ."

Pongwiffy stretched out a bony finger, then snatched it back hastily, unprepared for the sudden transformation. Hugo had shot to his feet, back arched and fur bristling. His lips were curled back in a snarl, exposing rows of wicked-looking little teeth, and a deep growl rumbled and throbbed in his small throat. If he had had a tail to speak of, it would have lashed. He didn't, so instead he lashed his whiskers. He was indeed an awesome sight.

Pongwiffy eyed him uneasily. After a moment, he gave a little shake, his fur flattened, his whiskers subsided, and he sat down and scratched his left ear with his right hind leg. Pongwiffy wondered if she had imagined it.

"You 'ave sumpsink to eat?" he asked. "Little bit of carrot? Apple, maybe? I come a long way from 'ome."

"No," said Pongwiffy. "Go away. The interview's over."

" 'Ow can zis be? You 'ave not asked me questions."

Pongwiffy sighed. It was getting late, and she still hadn't had her supper. This pushy Hamster was beginning to get on her nerves.

"Now listen," she snapped. "Put yourself in my place—er . . ."

" 'Ugo. Viz an *H*."

"Yes, yes, whatever your silly name is. Now, how do you think it would look if I turned up at the next Sabbat with you in tow? I'd die of embarrassment. All the others will be there with their Familiars . . ."

"Uzzers? Vat uzzers?"

"The other Witches in the Coven. Thirteen of us, including me. That's the right number for a Coven, you know."

"Tell me about zem," said Hugo, sounding interested.

"Well now, there's Grandwitch Sourmuddle, of course, she's Mistress of the Coven. Her Familiar's a Demon, name of Snoop. Then there's Sharkadder, my best friend, she's got Dead Eye Dudley. Cats are always popular as Familiars. Agglebag and Bagaggle—that's the twins— they've got Cats too, Siamese ones, IdentiKit and CopiCat. Witch Macabre, she's got that hideous Haggis creature, Rory. Bendyshanks, now, she's got a Snake, and Gaga—well, she's Bats, of course. Sludgegooey's got this Fiend called Filth, he plays the drums, you know. Then there's Bonidle, she's got a Sloth. Scrofula's got a Vulture, Greymatter's got an Owl, and Ratsnappy's got a Rat. I think that's everybody."

"Except you. You 'ave nussink."

"Yes, and I'd sooner have nussink than a Hamster, thanks very much. The very idea!"

"Ah. But me, I am not just any 'amster."

"All Hamsters are the same to me, kiddo. Now off you go, there's a good little chap. You've wasted enough of my time. Run away and be somebody's pet."

A piercing scream of anguish shattered the peace of the night. Twirling around on the spot, Pongwiffy clamped her hand to her left earlobe, which had developed a sharp, agonizing pain. It was the sort of pain you might get if a small Hamster was attached by its teeth to your ear. That sort of pain.

"Ah, ah, ah, ah, ah!" gasped Pongwiffy in breathless little screams, hopping on the spot and flapping vainly at the small dangling bundle of fur just outside her vision. "Ah, ah, AH! LEGGO! GERROFF! GERROFF!"

Hugo hung on.

"LEGGO, I say! LET GO, OR I'LL PUT YOU THROUGH THE MINCER! I WILL, I'M WARN-ING YOUUUUUUUU . . ."

Hugo hung on.

"DO YOU WANT TO BE A HAMSTER-BURGER? DO YOU? AH, AH, AH, AH!" Pongwiffy danced around, braying piteously through gritted teeth.

Hugo hung on.

"Please!" whimpered Pongwiffy, changing tack, begging now. "Let go and I'll give you crumbs! Hundreds of 'em. I'll give you an apple core, promise! PROMISE!"

Hugo hung on.

Pongwiffy danced around the room a bit more. The Toad-in-the-Hole clapped, enjoying her performance.

"I'LL PUT A SPELL ON YOU! I WILL! JUST YOU WAIT!" raged Pongwiffy, and searched her brains for a spell to dislodge Hamsters from earlobes. The search was in vain. Her brain was empty of all but one word. The word said PAIN.

"What is it you want? What? WHAT?" sniveled Pongwiffy with tears in her eyes.

"Trial," said Hugo, as distinctly as he could through a mouthful of earlobe. "Proper trial. Zen you decide if I goot or not."

"All right, all *right*! You've got it! Pax! I give in."

To her intense relief, Hugo's jaws unclenched and he plopped lightly on to her shoulder.

"So sorry," he said politely, then scuttled down her arm and jumped to the floor where he nosed about looking for more crumbs.

Pongwiffy leaped to the sink and began dabbing at her smarting ear with a dirty rag. Her cheeks were flushed with the shame of it. She was glad there had been no witnesses. She wouldn't like it spread about that Pongwiffy had been attacked by a crazed Hamster. She didn't count the Toad. She should have. He spread it around something shocking when he recovered from his ordeal some time later.

Meanwhile, Hugo went snuffling about beneath the piles of broken crockery, stuffing his pouches with any food he could find.

The Toad took advantage of the situation, escaping through a crack in the door and hopping off into the night leaving small puddles of batter.

"Blackmail. Blackmailed by a Hamster!" snarled Pongwiffy, dabbing at the teeth marks.

"Ya," agreed Hugo cheerfully, emerging from beneath a cracked plate with a blackened toast crust in his paw. "But is your own fault. You say zat vord I no like."

"What word?"

"Pet. 'Ugo is not Pet. Let me tell you sumsink." Hugo settled himself comfortably on the rug in front of the fire and gnawed at the toast as he talked.

"Vere I come from, all ze 'amsters is pets. Ze 'ole of mine family become ze pets. Bruzzers, sisters, muzzer, fazzer, pets, pets, all of zem pets. Is disgrace. Make me mad."

"Where do you come from?" asked Pongwiffy curiously.

"Amsterdam. Vere you sink? Anyway, all my family are livink in ze cage, running around on ze stupid veel all day. Vat a life. Sometimes zey get taken out for cuddle. Not me. Zey try to cuddle me, zey get bite, no problem. I not pet material."

"You can say that again," muttered Pongwiffy, searching for a tube of Instant Cure-All.

"So, I make plans," continued Hugo. "I vork on ze muscles, plenty nuts, push-ups, vork-outs on ze veel, you know. Zen, von night, I am strong. Bend back bars and set out to seek ze fortune. I 'ave many adventures. You vant to 'ear?"

"No," said Pongwiffy, sulkily, still rummaging. "I am in great pain."

"Is goot story. You vill like. Ze Champion 'Amster escapes from ze cage to fight for ze Great Cause."

"What Great Cause?"

" 'Amsters Are Angry."

"Are they? I can't say I've noticed."

"Zey vill be. Soon as zey 'ear about ze missed job opportunities."

"What job opportunities?"

"Vitch Familiar."

"Now look. About that . . ."

"Look, I vant no arguments, okay? I 'ave—ow you say—set my 'eart on it. Trial is agreed. Tell me about ze job."

Pongwiffy sighed. She had just noticed that her supper was missing its vital ingredient, her ear hurt, the Instant Cure-All was missing and she was too tired to argue anymore.

"Oh—all right. If I must. Well, you'll have to help me with my spells, of course. And run messages. Bit of spying, that sort of thing. Telling on people."

"Vonderful!" said Hugo enthusiastically. " 'Ugo like to squeal."

"But I'm only trying you out, mind. And you'll have to do exactly as I say. You're not at all what I had in mind, you know."

"You not 'ave big choice. I ze only applicant, ya?"

"Ah," replied Pongwiffy. "But I expect loads will turn up tomorrow."

"Zat I doubt," said Hugo. "You are most smelly, if you don't mind my mentionink it."

"Not at all. Thanks," said Pongwiffy, flattered.

"Vat I call you? Pong?"

"Certainly not. That's much too over-familiar for a Familiar. You're not much more than a servant really, you know. You must call me O Mistress."

"Okay," agreed Hugo cheerfully. "Now. Vere I am goink to sleep, O Mistress?"

"How should I know? Somewhere where I'll step on you when I get out of bed tomorrow morning," said Pongwiffy spitefully.

Secretly, though, she rather liked being called O Mistress. It had a certain ring to it.

CHAPTER FOUR

THE TRIAL

Hugo's Trial was, to Pongwiffy's surprise, not as big a trial as she thought it was going to be. He made himself useful in a dozen different ways, and didn't take up much room. He took to Magic like a duck takes to water, having a good nose for where to find the right ingredients and shouting encouraging, admiring things like, "Ya! Zat vas a corker, zat vas!" when Pongwiffy conjured up pink explosions in the air or turned herself into a jar of Marmite. He was thrilled with the simplest spells, and Making Magic was more fun, somehow, when he was around.

Pongwiffy found herself beginning to enjoy his company in the evenings. He was a born storyteller—some might say fibber—and would entertain her for hours with his tales of Ze Escape From Ze Cage, Ze Fight Viz Ze Mountain Lion, Ze Voyage Around Ze Cape Of Death, and so on. In fact, by the end of the week, she had grown rather attached to him and found herself thinking that Hamsters made rather good Familiars, if Hugo was anything to go by.

However, there was one very big problem.

How was she going to explain him to the other Witches? Imagine confessing to having a Hamster as a Familiar. It didn't bear thinking about.

She rather hoped that Hugo wouldn't insist on coming to the monthly Sabbat which was to be held next Friday night on Crag Hill. She worried about it all week, then came up with a plan. The plan was to Sneak Out Very Quietly. It might have worked too, except that Hugo Sneaked first. He had crept into her hat, rightly suspecting foul play. He was so small and light that Pongwiffy didn't even feel him sitting on her head.

Congratulating herself, she mounted her Broom and rode through the night, chuckling as she thought of Hugo curled up fast asleep in the tea cozy he used for a bed. She could stop worrying about the problem for another month. By then, maybe she would have thought of something.

After a long, chilly ride, Crag Hill loomed before her. Pongwiffy zoomed in and left her broom gossiping with the others in the Broom park.

"Ve 'ave touchdown?" demanded a familiar voice, close to her ear. "Vat 'appens now?"

Pongwiffy nearly collapsed with the shock. She snatched off her tall hat and peered into the gloomy depths. Hugo's beady little eyes gazed up, full of excitement.

"Who said you could come?" she hissed furiously. "Did I say you could come? Did I? Did I say . . ."

"Yoo-hoo! Is that you, Pong?" That was Shark-adder.

Pongwiffy hastily rammed her hat back on.

"Stay in here and keep quiet," she snapped. "Or else!"

"Ven I get introduced?"

"Never. Later. Maybe. We'll see. Now SHHHH." To her relief, Hugo shushed. Pongwiffy walked through the trees and went to join Sharkadder, who was roasting beetles in the embers of a merrily blazing bonfire.

Nearby, the Witches Sludgegooey and Bendyshanks were busily making sandwiches and setting them out on trestle tables. There was a choice of three fillings—spiderspread, frog paste or fleas and pickle. Gaga, as usual, was hanging upside down from a tree with her Bats, who lined the branches like rows of old black socks. Scrofula and Ratsnappy were swapping knitting patterns, Bonidle was asleep, and Greymatter was composing a poem and sipping thoughtfully from a glass of dirty pond water. That only left Grandwitch Sourmuddle, Agglebag and Bagaggle, and Macabre to be accounted for—but they were always the last to arrive.

Elsewhere, the Familiars were chatting in little groups. Scrofula's Vulture was talking about a personal problem to Filth the Fiend, who was tapping out drum rhythms on a tree stump with his eyes closed, not really paying attention. Bonidle's Sloth was slumped in a pile of leaves, snoring every bit as loudly as his mistress. He didn't have a name—Bonidle couldn't be bothered to give him one—and the Sloth was too apathetic to even care.

Seething Steve, a small grass snake and Bendyshank's Familiar, was moonbathing on a rock, pretending not to care that he wasn't poisonous. Greymatter's Owl, whose name was Speks and who was intelligent, was talking to Ratsnappy's Rat, whose name as Vernon and who wasn't. He was good at mazes, though.

"Hello, Pong. Have a beetle," said Sharkadder gaily. She was dressed up to the nines in her smartest rags. She was wearing her greenest lipstick and her longest spiderleg false eyelashes. Squiggly strands of greasy hair hung like potato peelings down her back. She had evidently been at the hedgehogs again.

Dead Eye Dudley lounged at her feet, flicking

his tail and giving everyone dirty looks out of his single yellow eye. He spat rudely as Pongwiffy approached, then wandered off to strike fear into the hearts of his fellow Familiars, who buttered him up and called him Cap'n.

"Now then, Pong," said Sharkadder. "Tell me. Did you get a lot of replies to our advertisement?"

"Er . . . well, not a *lot*," said Pongwiffy uncomfortably. "Actually."

"How many?" pressed Sharkadder.

"One," said Pongwiffy. "Actually." She felt Hugo stir eagerly under her hat.

"Well? Did you hire it?"

"No," said Pongwiffy, and came out in green spots. This always happened when she told fibs. Just as well, or she'd tell them all the time.

"Well—it's sort of on trial. Actually," she amended hastily, and the spots died down.

"Did you bring it with you?"

"No. OUCH!" The green spots reappeared, and Pongwiffy did an odd little hop as Hugo gave her a warning nip. "I mean yes."

Sharkadder stared curiously, and Pongwiffy pretended she was trying out a new dance step.

"Well where is it then?" snapped Sharkadder. "What's the big secret? Is it a ferret or a weasel or what? Is it over by the Brooms?" She was peering around curiously, hoping to spot an unfamiliar face.

"Now?" whispered Hugo.

"What was that?" demanded Sharkadder suspiciously. "A squeak came from under your hat."

"Oh *really?*" said Pongwiffy with a casual yawn. "Actually , I think you must be mistaken, Sharky. Look, you've still got a hedgehog roller in. It must have been that."

"It was nothing of the sort! You've got something under there, Pongwiffy, and if it's your new Familiar you might at least be polite enough to introduce me. Seeing as I did the advertisement for you." Sharkadder stamped her foot crossly.

"Well—all right, Sharky, I do have something under there," confessed Pongwiffy. "But I'd sooner keep it under my hat for now, ha ha."

"Why?" persisted Sharkadder.

"Er—too terrifying. It'll scare you." Back came the green spots.

"Nonsense! You're lying to me, Pongwiffy, I can tell. In fact, there's this rumor going around, you know. Dudley heard it from a Toad . . ."

"Oh look! There's old—er—you know. Must have a word with her!" cried Pongwiffy, and scuttled off.

"I'll break friends!" shouted Sharkadder after her. Pongwiffy pretended not to hear, and made for the trestle tables. She snatched a sandwich and popped it under her hat for Hugo. Eating was the only thing that kept him quiet.

"You're not supposed to start on them yet," said Bendyshanks in a bossy voice. "Not till Grandwitch Sourmuddle arrives. You know The Rules. And why did you put it under your hat?"

"Mind your own business," said Pongwiffy rudely. "What would you rather I did? Pushed it up your nose?"

Now, that is just the sort of rude comment that is sure to start an argument—so it was just as well that at that very moment, there was an interruption. A terrible squawling noise rent the air. Imagine a hundred cats all having their tails pulled at the same time. It was rather like that, but worse.

"Jumpink gerbils!" exclaimed Hugo, in his dark, stuffy cone. "Vat in ze vorld is 'appenink?"

"Sssh. Stop scrabbling! It's Grandwitch Sourmuddle." And Pongwiffy stood to attention, along with everyone else.

From out of the pine trees came a small procession. First came Agglebag and Bagaggle, the identical twins, playing their violins. The noise they made was a cross between a dentist's drill and a cow with severe stomachache. They practiced every night to achieve this effect, and had it off just perfect. IdentiKit and CopiCat twined identically in and out of their legs.

Behind them came Witch Macabre in her ceremonial tartan rags. She was riding on her Haggis—an odd-looking creature called Rory with a great deal of shaggy fur and a daft-looking ginger fringe which hung down over its eyes, causing it to trip up every third or fourth step. To add to the racket, Witch Macabre was playing her bagpipes, breaking off every so often to shout, "Oot o' the way, ye sassanachs! Make way foor Wee Grandwitch Sourmuddle, Mistress o' the Coven!"

Grandwitch Sourmuddle tottered along vaguely at the rear, wondering what she was doing there. She was so old, she tended to forget things. On her

shoulder sat Snoop, her demon Familiar, looking bored.

The procession came to a halt before the bonfire. Agglebag and Bagaggle played their final earsplitting chord with a flourish, and the drone of the bagpipes wheezed to a halt. There was a general sigh of relief, and everyone waited respectfully for the Grandwitch to speak her important first words.

"Where am I?" she said. Snoop whispered in her ear.

"Yes, yes, I can see *that*, Snoop. I can see I'm on Crag Hill. But what's the occasion? My birthday or something? Where's the cake?"

"It's the monthly Sabbat, Grandwitch. You're supposed to do your speech," Snoop reminded her, as he always did.

"Speech, you say? What, before I blow out the candles?"

"There are no candles. There is no cake. Just the usual meeting," said Snoop patiently.

"They could have made me a cake. Mean old hags," whined Sourmuddle.

"It's not your birthday. Just the usual meeting."

The assembled throng yawned and shuffled, rather hoping Grandwitch Sourmuddle would retire soon.

"Do your speech. Then we can have the sand-wiches," suggested Snoop.

"Sandwiches? That's all there ever is, stale old sandwiches. Oh well, better get started I suppose. Hail, Witches!"

"Hail!" came the response, and as always a small cloud came hurtling through the night sky and delivered a short, sharp burst of hailstones before scuttling off again in a northerly direction.

"I declare this supermarket open," announced Sourmuddle, digging hailstones out of her ears. There was an uncertain pause while Snoop whis-pered again, making impatient gestures with his small, green webbed hands.

"Sorry. Sabbat. I declare this Sabbat open."

"Hooray!" shouted the Witches, and fell upon the sandwiches. Snoop tutted and spoke urgently into Sourmuddle's ear.

"Oh. Right. HOLD IT!"

Agglebag and Bagaggle played a single, impor-tant sounding discord on their violins, and Witch Macabre raised her bagpipes threateningly to her lips. The Haggis blew the fringe out of his eyes and gave a warning cough. Everyone stood stock-still, sandwiches half in and half out of mouths.

"News time first," ordered Sourmuddle. "Then

I cut the cake. Now, has anyone got any news we should all hear? Any new spells? Anyone done anything particularly horrible to a Goblin? No? Right then, in that case . . ."

"Wait!" Sharkadder pointed an accusing finger at Pongwiffy, who guessed what was coming and cringed.

"Pongwiffy's got some news!" announced Sharkadder in a clear, firm voice. "She's hired a new Familiar."

Everyone turned and looked at Pongwiffy. The Familiars rustled and flapped and looked expectant.

"Eh? Oh. Well, come on then, Pongwiffy, but make it snappy. I want to open my birthday presents. Up to the fire."

Wishing the ground would open up and swallow her, Pongwiffy slowly walked toward the fire, which is where you have to stand if you have news to tell. Under her hat, Hugo busily attended to his whiskers and brushed the crumbs from his chin. He wanted to look smart for his first appearance.

"Go on, Pong!" called Sharkadder in a mean sort of way. "Don't be shy. Introduce us to your Familiar."

Twelve white bony faces stared at Pongwiffy expectantly.

"She says it's terrifying. That's all she'd tell me. Although I used to be her best friend and even wrote the advertisement for her," Sharkadder told the assembled company.

"Hurry up, Pong, we're all waiting!" clamored the audience.

For a brief moment, Pongwiffy considered saying a quick spell which would transform Hugo into a wolf or a lizard, anything that wasn't cute—but Witches aren't so easily deceived, and she knew that she'd never get away with it. She gulped and took a deep breath.

"Actually . . ." she said. "Actually, he's a bit shy."

"Show us! Show us! Show us your Familiar!" came the chant, and Sharkadder started a slow hand clap.

"I'd sooner not introduce him right now, if you don't mind . . ."

"Boo! Against The Rules!" Which it was. Witches have the right to know about each other's Familiars. That way, no one has an unfair advantage.

It was no good. Pongwiffy knew that her hour of doom was at hand. Better to get the whole embarrassing thing over and done with.

"All right!" she said sulkily. "If you must

know, he's under my hat. And he's a . . . he's a . . . actually, he's a Hamster."

There was a terrible, sickening pause which seemed to go on forever. Then—which was worse——The Laughter began. It started as titters. Little sniggers and snickers, and the odd tee-hee. Then came chuckles and chortles, followed closely by hoots and guffaws. The Witches cackled, cawed, jeered, scoffed, shrieked, bellowed, howled and gibbered. Witches hung on to each other for support. Witches banged their heads against nearby trees. Witches pointed shaking fingers at Pongwiffy then collapsed to the ground, clutching their sides and gasping for breath.

Oh, the shame of it.

Pongwiffy hung her head as the wave of derision rolled over her. She would never live it down. She would have to move hovel and go far, far away where nobody knew her.

And under her hat, Hugo's eyes began to turn red.

"A Hamster! Oh, I can't bear it!" howled Bendyshanks, rolling around in the leaves and kicking her legs in the air.

"Where is he? Show us your Hamster, Pongwiffy! Terrify us!" begged Sludgegooey.

The Familiars were exchanging superior sideways glances with each other. They wanted to laugh too, but were used to taking their cue from Dudley. And Dudley wasn't laughing. Dudley

was sneering. His single yellow eye blazed and his crooked tail whipped from side to side. Menacingly, he swaggered forward, muscles rippling.

"Well now, boys," he drawled. "A 'amster, be it? A 'amster seekin' to join the crew? What'll it be next, I asks meself? A Christmas tree fairy?"

The Familiars fell about laughing. Dudley raised a paw, and there was instant silence.

"Let's be havin' a look at this 'ere 'amster," continued Dudley. "Let's see what we'm up against. Must admit to bein' curious. Seems to me Witch Familiar bain't a suitable job for a 'amster. Weak, fluffy little things as a rule."

Crouched in the darkness of Pongwiffy's hat, Hugo was beside himself. How *dare* they laugh at him! And as for the owner of that sneering voice—just let him wait! Blind with rage, he threw himself at the walls of the hat, tearing at the lining with his sharp little teeth.

"Not a suitable job at all," came Dudley's hateful hiss again. "Seems to me this 'ere 'amster's got delusions of grandeur, lads, what say you? A kiddy's pet, that's more like what an 'amster should be."

That did it. From beneath Pongwiffy's hat came a shrill squeal of outrage. Both Witches and

Familiars took an involuntary step back, their mouths dropping open. Pongwiffy snatched off her tall hat and revealed what looked at first sight to be a maddened nailbrush on top of her head.

"This is Hugo," announced Pongwiffy. "He's from Amsterdam. And he doesn't like being called a pet, Dudley. Not one little bit."

Hugo descended in three easy steps—head to shoulder, shoulder to hand, hand to ground. He landed within inches of Dudley's nose. The firelight reflected red in his eyes. His whiskers were seething, his teeth were gnashing, his ears were flattened, his back was arched, his fur was standing on end. Cute he wasn't. Even Pongwiffy edged away from him.

Dudley, however, that tough, battle-scarred veteran, stood his ground. Slowly he licked his lips and smiled a thin, cold cat smile.

"Say zat again!" raged Hugo. "Say zat again,

you old bag of vind. Who you sink you is? I tell you vat you is. A bus for ze fleas, zat's vat! I see zem 'opping on and off from 'ere!"

A gasp went up from Witches and Familiars alike. Nobody ever spoke that way to Dudley.

"Well well," scoffed Dudley. "So it's mutiny, eh? Lookin' for trouble, are ye, little feller? Wantin' ter challenge the Cap'n. Well, I ought ter teach yer a lesson, I s'pose, but tain't right. You'm just too small. I bain't that much of a bully. I expect yer mummy'll spank yer bottom, save me the trouble. Go play on yer wheel sonny. Off with ye, before I change me mind. Go and be some little kid's pet." And with a sneer, Dudley turned his back and prepared to swagger away.

We all recognize that, don't we? It's almost exactly the same as that bloodcurdling howl invented by Pongwiffy when Hugo did his earring impression. Perhaps a little different. This time, Hugo had opted for the tail.

Dudley whirled around, shaking his head in pain and astonishment. Of course, the source of the agony was still behind him. He tried lashing his tail to shake Hugo off. Hugo merely bit harder. Dudley skittered backward, wriggling his rear end and roaring such dreadful piratical curses that even the Witches were shocked.

"Terrific isn't he?" said Pongwiffy proudly to Sharkadder, who was rooted to the spot, frozen with horror as she watched the contortions of her darling.

"Get off! Get *off me tail*, ye pint-sized pom-pom off a pirate's bobbly hat! I'll trim yer sails! I'll run ye aground! I'll scupper ye, rot me for a ship's biscuit else! I'll mangle ye with me binnacle! Meeeahhhhh!"

Hugo hung on.

"Threats don't work," explained Pongwiffy knowledgeably to the fascinated audience.

She was right. They didn't. Neither did the Running Up And Down Hill, the Leaping Into The Air, the Twisting Around In Circles or the rasped orders to the Lads to Come To His Aid. None of the Familiars was prepared to risk it. This little Hamster was quite something. He simply hung on and hung on with the sticking power of a limpet dipped in superglue—and finally, Dudley could take no more.

"All right! All right! May the whales whip yer whiskers out, what be it ye *want?*"

"Shay shorry," said Hugo through a mouthful of stringy tail.

"Shan't. Meaaaaaaaaah! All right, all right! I'm *sorry*, may ye be brained by a ship's biscuit!"

"Vat's my name?"

"Hugo, may ye be cuddled by an octopus!"

"Vat am I?"

"A Hamster! Leggo, may the stingrays kiss yer mother!"

"Vat else?"

"Pongwiffy's Familiar, may ye be splatted by a rusty anchor!"

"Vat am I not?"

"A pet. A pet, a pet, a PET. Now, GET OFF MY TAIL!"

And Hugo let go. There was silence on the hill. Nobody could quite believe what they had just witnessed. Dead Eye Dudley, ex-pirate and leader of the Familiars, had been defeated by a Hamster. Dudley, aware of the shocked eyes, muttered something about having a bad back, and slunk off to lick his wounds. Sharkadder scuttled off after him, crying, "I'll never speak to you again, Pongwiffy!"

Pongwiffy scooped Hugo up and held him triumphantly aloft. The Witches and their Familiars gave a great cheer and crowded in, full of admiration and congratulations, wanting to be the first to shake the new champion by the paw.

"He's small, I know," babbled Pongwiffy. "And sort of cute, I'm afraid. But he's got guts, and he does his best. That's what counts."

Hugo sat on her shoulder, shaking hands and trying to look casual. But inside, he was glowing. He'd made the grade. He'd struck a blow for Hamsters everywhere. His future was mapped out, and he had a real career before him.

"Vat about anuzzer sandvich?" he said.

"Not a chance," said Granwitch Sourmuddle, crawling out from beneath an empty trestle table. "I just finished the last one. And now I think it's time to cut my cake."

CHAPTER FIVE

LITTLE PIECES OF PAPER

"These Sabbats are really boring," complained Pongwiffy to Grandwitch Sourmuddle a few weeks later. "Nothing exciting's happened since Hugo put Dudley in his place. That was ages ago."

Sourmuddle unclamped her toothless gums from a stale spiderspread sandwich and said, "I'm sure this bread is left over from last month. I recognize the green speckly bits."

"That's what I mean. Even the food's awful. All we ever do is eat old sandwiches and swap old news. Dull. Dull-dull-dull. Dull as ditchwater."

"Ditchwater can be quit tasty at times. Depends what's swimming in it." Sourmuddle dug out a green speckle of mold with a dirty fingernail and tasted it experimentally. "Hmm. Definitely last month's, that."

"We should do something different. For a change," mused Pongwiffy. "We ought to rack our brains and think of ideas. Write them down on little pieces of paper and put them in a hat. I'm sure something would come out of it."

"I know what'd come out of it," said Grand-witch Sourmuddle wisely.

"What?"

"Little pieces of paper. Tee hee hee."

"Oh, there's no point in talking to you," snapped Pongwiffy crossly. "If you're happy to be mistress of the most boring Coven in the whole world, that's up to you. I suppose you can't help it if you're so old you don't like a bit of fun now and then."

"Me not like fun? Certainly I like fun, how dare you. I am a Fun-loving Person, and if you don't apologize I shall make your nose drop off. That'd be really funny."

"Sorry," said Pongwiffy sulkily. She was fond of her nose.

"What for?" said Sourmuddle, who had already forgotten. "What were we talking about?"

"How boring our Sabbats are," explained Pongwiffy patiently. "I was saying we should all put our heads together, and . . ."

"What, in a big pile, you mean? Then when the music stops we all rush in and grab one, and the one who doesn't . . ."

"No, no! I didn't mean that at all. It's just a figure of speech."

"Oh. Pity. It sounded fun," said Sourmuddle,

disappointed. "Though I'm not sure I know a head removing spell. Not offhand. You'd need your head screwed on to think of a spell like that. Tee hee hee."

Pongwiffy sighed. "Look, forget about the heads, Sourmuddle. I only meant that we ought to come up with some suggestions for interesting things to do."

"Oh, I *see*. To make the Sabbats less boring, you mean. Wait a minute! We could think of some things to do which would be fun, and have a really good time!"

"Exactly!'

"What a good idea. I might be getting on a bit, but I do come up with these good ideas from time to time."

"But it was my idea!" protested Pongwiffy.

"What was? Look, never mind about your idea now, Pongwiffy, let's concentrate on mine, before I forget it. Everyone must come up with some suggestions. We'll put them in a hat and have a vote. Well? What are you waiting for? Organize it!"

So Pongwiffy organized it. A moment later, all the Witches on Crag Hill were surprised to find little pieces of paper and sharp red pencils suddenly appear in their hands. They muttered uneasily, hoping it wasn't a spelling test.

Pongwiffy whisked Hugo away from an admiring group of Familiars, popped him on her shoulder and marched up to the bonfire.

"Quiet, everyone! I have something important to say. Grandwitch Sourmuddle and I have just been having a chat. These Sabbats are really boring, and my idea is this . . ."

"*My* idea!" interrupted Sourmuddle, stamping her foot. "Mine! Mine!"

"All right, then. Sourmuddle's-idea-which-she-pinched-from-me is this. Everyone has to come up with a suggestion and write it down and put it in my hat. Then we'll go through them, and decide on the best one."

"What sort of suggestions?" asked several voices at once.

"That's up to you. Anything you think might be fun."

"I know! I know!" screeched Witch Gaga. "We can all hang upside down from trees pretending to be bats. Or if it's a chestnut tree we can be nuts, or if it's a Christmas tree we can be crackers . . ."

"Yes, well, write it down, Gaga, write it down. Now, no more talking. You have exactly five minutes from NOW."

There was a great deal of panicky shuffling. Witches went into huddles with their Familiars, crying things like, "Stop looking! Macabre's trying to copy!" and "My pencil's broken!" and "How d'you spell bats?"

Five minutes later, Pongwiffy called time.

"Write your names on, then get in an orderly line. No pushing. Right, let's have your papers."

In a disorderly mob and with a great deal of pushing, the Witches dropped their papers into Pongwiffy's upturned hat then sat down again, looking expectant.

"Now then. Hugo will pass them to me one by one, and I shall read them out. Clap if you like any of the ideas. First please, Hugo."

Hugo dipped into the hat and passed the first paper to Pongwiffy. She smoothed it out and frowned.

"This is blank. Who handed in a blank piece of paper?"

"Me," confessed Bonidle with a bored yawn.

"But everyone's supposed to have an idea! You've written nothing."

"That's my idea. I like doing nothing. So there." And Bonidle promptly went to sleep.

"Well, I don't think much of that. Any claps for that one?"

There were no claps for that one, so Pongwiffy moved on to the next. "This one's Macabre's idea.

It says, *SING SCOTTISH BATTLE SONGS OR MUD WRESTLING.*"

"Aye. Ah thought o' two," bragged Witch Macabre, and her Haggis gave her an admiring lick with his long purple tongue.

"But we don't know any Scottish battle songs, Macabre. And this mud wrestling business, I don't think any of us here fancy it much."

"Aye, but ah do."

"Yes, Macabre, but you can't mud wrestle on your own, can you? Who'd win? The mud? Well, let's put it to the vote. Who wants to sing battle songs or mud wrestle with Macabre?" Nobody did, so she moved on.

"EVERYONE BRINGS A BALLOON AND POPS IT. That's the twins." Agglebag and Bagaggle hugged each other and giggled.

"Well, it's not *bad* I suppose," said Pongwiffy doubtfully. "Balloons are partyish sort of things . . ."

"No! No balloons! My granny got eaten by polar bears because of one of them balloons!" That was Sourmuddle.

"Dear, dear. Why was that?" enquired Pongwiffy politely.

"She collided with one of them hot air balloons she did, over the North Pole it was, punctured it with her broomstick she did, you could hear the explosion for miles around, you could. Or was that my great granny? Yes, come to think of it, it must have been great granny. Or was it someone else's granny? Fetch me another sandwich, Snoop. What was I saying?"

"Never mind," said Pongwiffy heavily. "No balloons. Next please, Hugo."

"Mine next," said Grandwitch Sourmuddle, suddenly remembering what was happening.

"It's not your turn . . ."

"Who's Mistress of this Coven? Mine next."

Muttering, Pongwiffy signaled to Hugo, who scrabbled around in the hat until he found Sourmuddle's paper.

"HAVE A BIRTHDAY PARTY FOR SOUR-MUDDLE," read out Pongwiffy, and a vast sigh went up.

"Well, why not?" whined Sourmuddle.

"Because your birthday's still two months away. You've been told a hundred times."

Sourmuddle went into a deep sulk, and Pongwiffy moved on.

The next idea was, *BRING-AND-BUY SALE.* That was from Bendyshanks. Everyone wanted to know what a Bring-and-Buy Sale was. Bendyshanks said they all had to bring a load of Old Rubbish and buy it. The Witches wanted to know what sort of Old Rubbish. Bendyshanks said rags, old shoes, homemade cakes and jigsaws with half the pieces missing. Ratsnappy growled that it seemed daft, coming up with a load of Old Rubbish then buying it straight back. Bendyshanks explained that the idea was to buy other people's Old Rubbish.

This provoked an outcry. Witches declared that they wouldn't be seen dead in one of Pongwiffy's stinky old cardigans or a pair of Sludgegooey's shoes. And as for Gaga's homemade sponge with the cement filling—talk about instant death, one slice of that and it'd be a Bring-and-Die Sale. And so on and so on.

The Bring-and-Buy Sale was obviously doomed to failure, so Pongwiffy moved on to the next idea, which was, *START A BROWNIE PACK*, suggested by Ratsnappy. This was roundly jeered, and quite right too.

Greymatter's *INTELYJENT SOCIETY FOR BRAINY WITCHES* didn't get a single clap because no one could spell Intelligent.

Scrofula's *RAFFLE* proved equally unpopular when it was discovered that the prize would be a rare collection of Scrofula's old hairbrushes. Scrofula's dandruff was shocking. She had the most Christmassy shoulders in the world.

Gaga's idea of *HANGING FROM TREES* never got written down, because she was off somewhere hanging from one. That meant there was now only one remaining paper in the heat. It belonged to Sharkadder.

Now, it must be remembered that Sharkadder was still sore about Hugo making her Dudley look foolish. Also, she had recently had another row with Pongwiffy. Something about missing hair rollers. In fact, she and Pongwiffy were currently worst enemies.

Sharkadder's paper said,

MAKE-UP DEMONSTRATION.

"Huh," said Pongwiffy, reading it out with a sneer. "Well, I think we all agree that's a terrible idea, so I'm afraid . . ."

"Hold it!" howled Sharkadder, outraged. "You haven't given anyone a chance to clap! You saw that, everyone, she didn't even . . ."

"Oh, all right. Hands up anyone who in their right mind would volunteer to be made up by Sharkadder. Bearing in mind she uses brillo pads for cleansing, which is why her own ugly mug looks like the surface of the moon. There, see, no one. Told you."

Sharkadder flexed her long nails dangerously

and said, "Not so fast, ferret face. There's another suggestion on the other side."

There was too. It said:

> TIE PONGWIFFY TO A THORN BUSH AND THROW OLD TEA BAGS AT HER!

"Suggest you do not read zis one out," advised Hugo in a whisper. " 'E might be popular." Pongwiffy took his advice and accidentally on purpose dropped the paper in the fire. Sharkadder jumped up and down, snarling.

"Well, that's that," said Pongwiffy, ignoring her. "What a load of useless suggestions. I don't know why I bothered."

"What about you, bug brain?" heckled Sharkadder. "What's your idea?"

"I don't have to think of one. I organized it."

"Boo!" howled the Witches, led by Sharkadder. "Can't think of one!"

"Can," snapped Pongwiffy, who couldn't. Her brains always seemed to be out whenever she called on them. Luckily, Hugo came to her rescue.

"I vish to speak." There was immediate silence. For a new boy, Hugo commanded a great deal of respect. In fact, he was already well on his way to becoming leader of the Familiars, particularly since Dudley was still on the sick list.

"My Mistress 'ave an idea. A great idea."

"I do? Oh—er—quite right," agreed Pong-wiffy. "You tell them, Hugo. I'm shy." And she listened with interest to what her idea was.

"*TALENT CONTEST*," announced Hugo. "Ze Great Talent contest. Ze vinner vill vin a vunder-ful avard vich I vill carve viz mine own paws. I shall call it ze 'Ugo Avard."

"Eh? What's he talking about?" muttered the Witches, having trouble with all this talk of vin-ners and avards.

"He means the best act gets a prize," trans-lated Pongwiffy. "I think."

"Not only zat," continued Hugo, warming to his subject and ignoring Pongwiffy, who was try-ing to shut him up. "As well as prize, ze contest vill be judged by A Famous Person from ze world of show business. Ve vill send out invitations far and vide. Zis contest vill go down in 'istory!"

There was an awed silence.

"Idiot!" hissed Pongwiffy.

Suddenly, to Pongwiffy's astonishment, the silence erupted into a storm of applause. A talent contest! Of course. With an award, and a Famous Person judging it! What a good idea!

• • •

"It's a terrible idea, you stupid Hamster!" screamed Pongwiffy, the minute they were at home and in private. "It's all very well for you. You go making all these rash promises, then I'm stuck with the consequences. A Famous Person from the world of show business my foot. Do *you* know anyone like that? I'm sure I don't. Except for a monkey I once knew who joined a circus, but I believe he's retired."

"No problem," said Hugo with a wink. He was sitting in a cracked teacup, making notes on the back of a postage stamp.

"Guess 'oo is at zis very moment 'olidaying at 'is castle retreat on ze uzzer side of Vitchvay Vood."

"How should I know? Who?"

"Scott Sinister. Zat's 'oo. Zat'll be anuzzer contribution to ze 'Amsters Are Angry cause, pliz." Hugo had begun charging for Good Ideas.

"*What?*" Pongwiffy ripped the sleeve off her cardigan in her excitement. "Scott Sinister? *The* Scott Sinister? Star of a thousand horror movies and *my dreamboat?*"

"Ze very same."

"Oh, Hugo! Just imagine if Scott Sinister would come and judge our talent contest! I'd meet him in the flesh! I've always loved hm, ever since I was a teenwitch. Oh, Scott, Scott." Pongwiffy went into a trance, a soppy grin on her face.

"Zere you are, zen. No problem."

"But how will we get him to agree? I mean, he's on holiday, isn't he? He might not want to. Oh Scott, Scott, I've lost you!"

"Nonsense. We persuade him."

"How? Gold? He's so rich he doesn't need it."

"Nein. Sumpsink better. Blackmail."

"*Blackmail?* Blackmail my Scott?"

"Ya."

Pongwiffy thought about it. "Hmm. Good idea," she said.

"Zat'll be twenty pence," said Hugo.

CHAPTER SIX

SCOTT SINISTER

Scott Sinister, Famous Star of stage and screen, and Pongwiffy's dreamboat, was reclining in a purple silk hammock by the side of the large, coffin-shaped swimming pool which took up most of the castle grounds. He was wearing a gold dressing gown with S S embroidered across the front. Expensive (but silly) sunglasses shaded his Famous Red Eyes, gold chains dripped from his Famous White Throat, and gold fillings flashed as he picked at his Famous Fangs with a gold-plated toothpick. His Famous Feet nestled in fur-lined snakeskin slippers, and diamonds the size of Ping-Pong balls sparkled on his Famous Fingers.

To one side of him, there was a table piled high with rare delicacies—sweet pickles from the Lost Isle of Pan Yan, bogberries from the Misty Mountains, mole-flavored yogurt, and a great bucket of gorilla ice cream. On the other side, a small grim-faced Gnome in turban and swimming trunks held up a large crimson umbrella to protect the Famous Flesh from the sun. The

Gnome also waved a fan around in a casual sort of way, giving the occasional slight clonk to the Famous Nose.

"Look, *do* you mind! Why can't you watch what you're doing?"

"Okay, bud, okay," said the Gnome, who was only temporary.

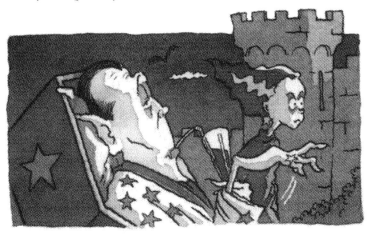

"I don't know what's happening to servants these days," grumbled Scott Sinister to the starlet who was gently dabbing at his brow with a cloth dipped in perfumed water. "Badness knows I pay them enough." He took a sip from a glass containing something red with ice cubes, and gestured despairingly with a limp white hand. "I mean, just look at those bodyguards.

What a bunch. That's what comes of hiring the locals."

The bunch consisted of several large Goblins in bobble hats, huge boots and grubby, tight-fitting dinner jackets. They stood around cracking their finger joints, fiddling with their bow ties and muttering in low voices. A bent, hump-backed figure in butler's uniform creaked about collecting dirty glasses. It was wearing a paper bag over its head(?). Two She-Goblins in blonde wigs sprawled by the side of the pool, lumpy bodies stuffed into pink bathing costumes, hoping to be in Scott Sinister's next film.

Just then, the biggest Goblin came up, obvi-

ously bursting with news. Guess who? Plugugly, no less! Small world, isn't it?

" 'Scuse me, Mr. Sinister," said Plugugly. "Dere's a 'amster at de main gate. Wants a word wiv yer."

"A *Hamster?* Bad gracious, Goblin, who do you think I am? I'm on holiday, remember? I have better things to do than talk to rodents. Do you have any idea what it's like to be rich and famous and extremely bad looking? Well, I'll tell you. It's exhausting. That toothpaste commercial was the last straw. I am tired, Goblin. Tired, weary, strained, tense, jaded, fagged, drained and totally pooped. I hired you to protect me from my adoring public, so go and do it! Hurry up, step on it!"

"Step on it? Right, sir."

Plugugly bowed as deeply as his belly would let him. All the buttons burst from his dinner jacket and rolled into the swimming pool. Plop, plop, plop, plop, plop. Plugugly waddled away, looking vexed.

"Now, perhaps I can relax a little. Lulu, my darling, pass me one of those marzipan frogs. No, on second thought, I think I'll have a nap.

I've already been up two hours, how much more can my body take? But first, pass me that mirror. I haven't looked at myself for ages. I've told you before, Gnome, keep that fan *moving!*"

Before Lulu could pass the mirror, Plugugly was back again, jacket flapping messily and a grubby looking envelope in his hand.

" 'Ate ter bovver yer again, Mr. Sinister, sir," he said. "I tried ter step on it, but it threatened to bite me. It give me a letter fer yer. It's waitin' fer a—what were it again? Oh yer—Reply."

"Stubborn little beast, isn't it? Oh, give it here, then. Fan mail I suppose."

"In that case, fan yourself with it," said the Gnome throwing down both umbrella and fan and walking out in a huff.

"That's right! Go sit by a pond somewhere, it's all you're fit for anyway! That's the last time I hire a Gnome. I'd sooner be gnomeless. Ha, ha, hear what I just said, Lulu?"

Pleased with himself, Scott Sinister slit the envelope with a filed fingernail and took out a filthy piece of paper. His good mood didn't last long. In Pongwiffy's best writing, the note said:

Dear Scott Sinister,

You don't no me, but i am yore biggest fan, I have sin all yore films. I liked you best as the daddy in The Mummy's Curse. Now, heer is my rekwest. Plese will you come and judge our talent contest in Witchway Hall next friday. I no you will agree to do this becos you are such a kind and Wunderfull persun. Also, I don't think you would like to wake up tomoro morning and find yore Wunderfull swiming pool full of dad rats.

Yore bigest fan,

Pongwiffy (witch)

p.s. Can I have yore autograrf?

"Blackmail! That's what it is! These Witches think they can get away with anything!" cried Scott Sinister, throwing down the letter in a fit of pique.

"Oh, I dunno," said Plugugly, picking it up and peering at it. "It's dirty, yer, but not exackly black. More gray. Yer, gray mail's what I'd call it."

He was quite surprised when he found himself at the bottom of the swimming pool. But at least he found two of his buttons.

• • •

"I shall frame it," said Pongwiffy happily, reread-
ing the letter from Scott Sinister for the ump-
teenth time that evening. "I shall hang it on the
wall over my bed and charge people to come and
look. Just think, Hugo. He touched this paper
with his own hands. Oh, Scott, Scott."

There was a knock on the door. Agglebag and
Bagaggle had come to enquire if it really was true
that Scott Sinister had agreed to judge the contest,
and please could they see the letter.

"Yes, it's true, and no you can't," said Pongwiffy. "Not unless you give me ten pence each.
Make that twenty and I'll let you touch it."

The twins humbly paid up and stood gazing at
the letter in awe. It was written on scarlet note-
paper with gold edging, and said, in big black
letters,

Dear Blackmailer,
I suppose so
Yours sincerely
Scott Sinister (✰)

"It doesn't say much, but I think he likes me," said Pongwiffy shyly. "See where he says he's mine sincerely?"

The next week was a waking nightmare. Pongwiffy's head was buzzing with all the things she had to think about and organize, and her hand nearly fell off with writing so many lists, all of which she lost.

"Hugo! Where's the list of acts? Here it is . . . no, that's a shopping list. Oh bother, I'm going to have to make a list of these lists . . ."

Calmly, Hugo handed her the list of acts. It was in alphabetical order and included the name of every Witch in the coven apart from Pongwiffy, who was the organizer, and wasn't taking part. It went like this:

Agglebag and Bagaggle : A Moosikal Dewet
Bendyshanks : Tap Dansing on Roler Skates
Bonidle : Koodunt Kare Less
Gaga : Mad Histirikal Laffing
Greymatter : A Pome
Macabre : Sumthing Scottish
Ratsnappy : Funy Jokes
Scrofula : Ventrillokwissum
Sludgegooey : Impbreshuns
Sharkadder : Mak-up Demonstrayshun
Sourmuddle : A seekret Song

Pongwiffy examined it doubtfully. "You know, I'm not at all sure about Gaga's act. Mad, hysterical laughing. She does that all the time anyway."

"Ah, but not in costume," pointed out Hugo.

"Hmm. Where's my list? The one with all my duties on?"

Hugo handed it to her. It said:

PONGWIFFY:

Stayg Manijer, Prodowser
Moosikal Direktor   Props
Programs   Liting
Box Ofiss   Compair
Poblissity   Everything Else

"It's no good," said Pongwiffy, looking at it. "I simply can't cope." And she couldn't. The responsibility of it all and the thought that she was to meet Scott Sinister in the flesh proved too much. She wasted a lot of time making a frame for The Letter, then made herself sick with excitement and had to go to bed.

Hugo took over. He held a meeting with the other Familiars, but they didn't waste time making lists. Instead, they got right out and did the job—some of them providing the brains and others the brawn. They organized the benches in

Witchway Hall, ordered the Brooms to sweep the stage, got the lights working, stopped the curtains sticking, had the piano tuned, got the programs and *NO GOBLINS* posters printed, sold the tickets, ordered the ice cream and booked the band.

All these things could have been done by Magic if the Witches had been prepared to put their minds to it—but they were far too busy rehearsing their acts to worry about such dull, practical matters. The smell of greasepaint was in the air, and they all had visions of receiving the Hugo Award from Scott Sinister's own hands (to thunderous applause, naturally).

Some of them took to wearing dark glasses and claiming that they wanted to be alone, in between trying to get themselves photographed for the *Daily Miracle*. Even Bonidle entered into the spirit of things, changing her act from *KOODUNT KARE LESS* to *UNICYCLING*. No one had seen the unicycle, but she could be seen from time to time limping home from some secret place swathed in bandages.

All the Witches kept their acts a close secret. You might have heard a few mysterious noises coming from various caves and cottages as you strolled through the wood, but that was all.

Nobody really knew what anyone else was doing, and the atmosphere was charged with tension and excitement. Pongwiffy, meanwhile, lay in bed cuddling The Letter and counting the minutes.

"I make it only another two thousand eight hundred and eighty-two to go, Hugo," she said dreamily some days later. Hugo was putting the final touches to the Hugo Award, which was a small statue of a Hamster holding a torch aloft. It was rather good except that the gold paint tended to rub off (being cheap cut-price stuff from Macabre's uncle, who was in the trade).

"Two tousant eight 'undred and eighty-two vat?"

"Minutes to go. Till I meet Scott Sinister."

"Oh ya? Sumpsink up wiz your maths, I sink."

"Why? How many do you make it?"

"Sixty."

"WHAT! You're wrong, you must be!"

"Is true. Is now fifty-nine. You 'ave been fast asleep for two days. Better get out of bed. Tonight's ze night!"

He was right. It was. Pongwiffy nearly died.

Witchway Hall was packed. News of the Great Talent Contest had spread far and wide, and the tickets had been snapped up like hotcakes. A party of Skeletons had arrived in a hired hearse, talking loudly in snooty voices about the poor quality of entertainment on offer these days. Nevertheless they sat in the most expensive seats.

There was a bit of fuss when ticket holders found their seats already occupied by Ghouls who had sneaked in through the walls when nobody was looking, but Dead Eye Dudley was the bouncer, and managed to sort it out to everyone's dissatisfaction.

A row of Banshees shrieked and howled to each other in the back row, passing sweets and ignoring the glares from the rest of the audience. Fiends, Demons, Trolls, Bogeymen, Werewolves and even a couple of Wizards (in disguise, of course—it wouldn't do to be seen at a Witch Do) packed the hall.

The band began to tune up. They were called the Witchway Rhythm Boys, and consisted of a small Dragon named Arthur who played the piano, a Leprechaun named O'Brian on penny whistle and Filth the Fiend on drums. They were a long time tuning up, and the audience were getting restless.

"Why don't you play a proper tune?" screamed one of the Banshees in the back row.

"We just did," said Arthur.

Meanwhile, Pongwiffy was biting her fingernails outside the hall. The Guest of Honor and Judge of the contest still hadn't arrived. Suppose he didn't turn up. Suppose he was ill, or his coach had broken down or he'd lost the address or forgotten the day or . . . Suddenly, her heart leapt at the welcome sound of drumming hooves and a cracking whip.

Into the glade galloped a team of plumed, snorting, sweating coal black horses, towing behind them a long, low, gaudily painted coach. A huge star decorated the door, and the number plate read S S 1. Scott Sinister had arrived!

Pongwiffy gave a muffled little scream of excitement as the coachman—a bent, humpbacked figure with a paper bag over its head(?), shuffled around to the door and wrenched it open with a flourish. Out stepped the great man, wearing an imposing gold and scarlet cloak, black fingerless gloves (to show off the rings) and a pair of rather silly sunglasses. Moonlight glinted off his sharp white teeth and his swinging medallions.

Pongwiffy stepped forward and dropped a deep, wobbling curtsy. Her heel caught in her hem, and there was a nasty tearing sound. It didn't matter—holes were a feature of the dress.

"Mr. Sinister—may I call you Scott? I feel I

know you so well. Scott, this is indeed an honor. I am Witch Pongwiffy, your humble fan."

"Hmm. So you're the hag who threatened to put rats in my pool," said Scott Sinister coldly.

"I am," confessed Pongwiffy. "But I wouldn't have done it, you know. Not really. I think you're wonderful. It seemed the only way to get you here. So let's forget all about it, I don't want anything to spoil this wonderful moment."

Just then, something did spoil the wonderful moment. Lulu the starlet stepped from the coach, dripping with jewels and wearing a white evening gown. She was followed by Plugugly, with whom, as we know, Pongwiffy has had dealings in the past.

"My entourage," said Scott Sinister haughtily. "I never go anywhere without them."

"Oh? Well that's a pity, Scott, because, you see, we don't allow Goblins in Witch Territory."

Pongwiffy gave her Wand a casual little wave, and Plugugly vanished with a howl of protest. All that was left of him was a sad little pile of buttons and an egg-stained bow tie, which fluttered to the ground like an ailing butterfly.

"Darling, who is this smelly old woman?" enquired Lulu, fluttering her eyelashes.

"Pongwiffy. Hello," said Pongwiffy rudely,

waving her Wand again. Lulu disappeared with a startled little scream. Her jewels remained behind, however, and Pongwiffy picked them up and popped them into her pocket—just for safe keeping, naturally.

"We have a rule about stuck-up hussies in nighties, too," she explained to Scott Sinister, who had gone *really* pale. "Isn't this nice? I've got you all to myself." And linking her arm with his, she propelled him firmly toward the hall.

There was a great deal of oohing and ahhing, nudging and whispering and scattered applause as Pongwiffy, bursting with pride, escorted the famous star up the gangway to the seat of honor slap in the middle of the front row. You could tell it was the seat of honor because it was the only one with a cushion.

Scott Sinister swallowed hard as he peered around at the assembled audience. He was used to horrifying sights in his profession, but never had he seen such a grisly mob as this. To give him his due, though, he kept his head, and managed a limp wave and a bow or two before Pongwiffy shoved him impatiently into the special chair. There he sat, chewing his nails nervously, wondering what he'd let himself in for.

Pongwiffy scuttled up to the stage and began what was intended to be a very long opening speech.

"Ladies and Gentlemen, Fiends, Demons and Bogeymen, lend me your ears," she said importantly. "Thank you for coming. We're very honored to have here tonight, Mr. Scott Sinister, who will judge the first ever Witch Talent Contest to be held in the history of the universe."

"Hooray!" enthused the audience, throwing crisp bags around.

"It was me who thought of getting him, you know," went on Pongwiffy. "In fact, this whole talent contest which you are about to enjoy was my idea, and I'd just like to say a few words about how I . . ."

"Boo!"

"Siddown"

"Gerronwivit!"

"Oh, all right," said Pongwiffy sulkily. "Have

it your own way. Is the first act ready back there, Hugo?"

A muffled squeak came from behind the closed curtains.

"Right. Well, the first act is Agglebag and Bagaggle, who will play a musical duet. Take it away, boys!"

The Witchway Rhythm Boys took it away and played a few bars of something rather horrible. Pongwiffy scurried to her chair which was set in the wings, the houselights dimmed, and the Great Talent Contest finally began.

CHAPTER SEVEN
THE CONTEST

The curtains creaked apart to reveal the twins standing side by side stage center, violins beneath their chins. They were wearing identical spotted scarves tied gypsy fashion around their brows, identical patched swirly skirts and identical terrified expressions of stage fright. There was a long silence, and nothing happened. The audience sniggered unkindly.

"Get on with it!" hissed Pongwiffy from the wings. "Do something, idiots." Each twin gave an identical nervous cough and an identical nervous shuffle. They nudged each other several times, and finally, much to everyone's relief, Agglebag spoke.

"This is a song about Witchway Wood. Sh-She wrote the words."

"And sh-she wrote the music," added Bagaggle.

"I sing the first verse, and she plays v-violin."

"And I sing the second, and *she* plays v-violin." They hesitated a moment, and looked at each other.

"But first, we both play violin," they chorused

together, and did. It was awful, but then it always was. After scraping away together a bit, Agglebag lowered her violin and sang her verse in a throaty voice.

"Witchway Wood is really good," sang Agglebag.

"Doo witchy doo witchy doo," sang Bagaggle, scraping away.

Much much better than Christmas pud," sang Agglebag.

"Doo witchy doo witchy doo," obliged Bagaggle, then they both leapt about a bit, doing what they assumed were gypsyish movements, swirling their skirts and stamping. Then Bagaggle sang her verse.

"Witchway Wood is where I'll be," she trilled.

"Doo witchy doo witchy doo," caroled Agglebag, scraping. Then there was a pause.

"I've forgotten the next bit, Ag," confessed Bagaggle, and burst into tears.

"Hooray!" thundered the audience in relief, and clapped their approval. The twins, assuming the applause meant they had gone down well, curtsied shyly and skipped off with their arms around each other while Hugo closed the curtains.

"Didn't we do well?" they asked Pongwiffy.

"Hmmm," said Pongwiffy doubtfully, and went to announce the next act. This was Bendyshanks' roller-skating tap dance.

The Witchway Rhythm Boys struck up, the curtains wobbled open, Filth played an impressive drumroll, and Bendyshanks zoomed on stage. There was a lot of smoke coming from her heels. In fact, they appeared to be seriously on fire. She was wearing a crash helmet, and her bandy old legs sported red, white and blue shin pads.

The audience only had a fleeting glimpse of the outfit, however, for not only did Bendyshanks zoom on stage, she zoomed straight off it again, falling like a stone straight into the orchestra pit where the Witchway Rhythm Boys were playing Roller Skating Tap Dance Music.

Her head went straight through Filth's drum and she had to be carried out with her thin little legs in their jolly shin pads kicking feebly in the air. At least everyone got a good look at the Special Custom Built Super Charged Roller Skates with Attached Rocket Launcher, just before they exploded. When they did, the audience went wild. Scott Sinister yawned and looked at his watch.

"Bonidle will now perform on her Unicycle," announced Pongwiffy over the uproar. Everyone sat up, interested, for nobody had yet seen the famous Unicycle.

When it finally wobbled from the wings, with Bonidle precariously perched on top, it was indeed an impressive sight, consisting mainly of an old cart wheel with a makeshift seat arrangement tied somehow on the top with string. However, the best bit was undoubtedly the handlebars.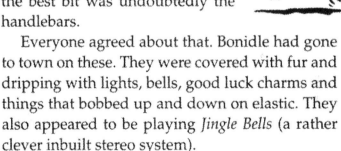

Everyone agreed about that. Bonidle had gone to town on these. They were covered with fur and dripping with lights, bells, good luck charms and things that bobbed up and down on elastic. They also appeared to be playing *Jingle Bells* (a rather clever inbuilt stereo system).

The only thing they didn't have was brakes. Bonidle hadn't bothered to fit any, having lost interest toward the end. This was rather a pity, because there's little point in wasting long, painful hours mastering the Art of Balance unless you also master the Art of Stopping.

Bonidle merely rolled relentlessly onward,

ending up (you've guessed it) in the orchestra pit, together with her unicycle which promptly came adrift. Another drum was ruined, O'Brian's penny whistle got bent, Bonidle was carried off for first-aid treatment muttering, "Who cares anyway?" and the audience brought the roof down. Scott Sinister closed his eyes.

"The next act is Mad Hysterical Laughing from Gaga," announced Pongwiffy, when order was once again restored. "I'm afraid." The audience looked puzzled. It sounded an odd sort of act.

It was. The curtains parted to reveal a huge cardboard box painted with wild, crazy colors, sitting in the middle of the stage. From this burst Gaga, decked in a very strange outfit of paper flowers, ribbons, and huge safety pins. She had a clothes peg on her nose and a basket of bananas on her head. What looked like large stuffed parrots swung from her ears, and her feet sported bright yellow wellington boots. The effect was most unusual.

The Mad Hysterical Laughing wasn't, though. It was exactly the same as always, just as Pongwiffy had predicted. After several minutes of watching Gaga prance about cackling and waving her yellow boots, Pongwiffy gave a signal, and the colorfully garbed performer, still doubled up with mirth, was forcibly removed by two of the larger Familiars. The audience, after hesitating, decided to give her a clap for originality, so that was all right. Scott Sinister, however, was fast asleep. We'll leave him like that, because he slept for a very long time. He even missed the ice cream in the interval.

"A poem by Greymatter, Our Very Own Thinking Witch," bawled Pongwiffy. "Thank goodness," she added to Hugo. "A bit of class won't hurt after that lot."

The Brains of the Coven walked on stage, poem in hand. Her Witch hat had been replaced by a mortar board. Grimly, she adjusted her glasses, and spoke in a stern, headmistressy way, which had everyone hiding their sweets and paying attention.

"Right, sit up straight. This poem is entitled, *Hard Words*. I suspect it's way beyond you, but I can't help being clever. So here goes.

HARD WORDS
Adenoids, apothecary,
Symbolize, constabulary,
Oxidize, preliminary,
Psychic Eskimo,
Peekaboo and barbecue
Here's a French one, rendezvous,
These are but a sample
Of the hardest words I know.

"Thank you. Goodnight." And Greymatter walked off to a storm of applause. Nobody had understood a word, but thought that if they clapped hard enough, everyone else would think they had.

Next came Macabre who, if you remember, was planning Something Scottish. The curtains opened, and the audience gasped. Macabre, whose uncle was in the paint trade, had painted a huge backcloth depicting a Scottish Glen. There was a lot of swirling purple (heather), swirling gray (sky), and yellow blobs (sheep—her uncle couldn't get white).

In the midst of this Highland Scene sat Macabre in full Scottish rigout, mounted on her Haggis, who had a ton of heather plaited into his orange fringe and was draped with much tartan.

His head sported a peculiar sort of hat thing which was apparently Traditional Haggis Ceremonial Headgear. He snorted and shook his fringe proudly, pawing the boards while Macabre, wearing so much clashing tartan that the audience saw squares for a week, blew into her bagpipes, intending to treat the assembled company to a rousing chorus of *Scotland the Brave*.

Unfortunately, a tragedy had occurred. Somebody had Sabotaged The Bagpipes. We won't say who, because it really was a terribly mean thing to do, and if we ever found out who it was we'd have to kick her out of this story in disgrace, which would be a pity. But the fact remains that Somebody (armed with a knitting needle or something similar) had attacked those bagpipes in the still of the night and punctured them very thoroughly. In fact, they had more holes than a fishing net.

The minute Macabre blew, they gave a sad little puffing wheeze and then gave in and died.

Macabre, taken aback, shook them, attempted the
kiss of life, then gave vent to such a disgraceful
stream of Scottish Bad Words that the audience
were enthralled. The Haggis, also outraged,
reared up, steam hissing from its nostrils, and let
out a bitter moo.

"Ah'll find oot!" raged Macabre, waving her
ceremonial sword aloft. "Ah'll find oot who mur-
dered ma wee pipes if it's the last thing ah do!"

And she hurled the useless bagpipes into the
audience. They landed on Scott Sinister, but he
didn't wake up. She whirled her Haggis and galloped off stage, howling doom and destruction.

What an act! What could follow that but the
interval? The audience fell upon the ice cream
with cries of delight and contentedly stuffed
themselves, talking about how much they were
enjoying it. These Witches could certainly put on
a show. Even the Skeletons said it wasn't bad,
they supposed.

Ten minutes later Pongwiffy called time and
the audience waded back to their seats through a
sea of bogberry ripple and buzzed excitedly as
the second half began.

The first act after the interval was Ratsnappy.
She was dressed as a clown in a shiny suit with
bobbles attached. She had done her best, but the

wide red smile painted on her face did little to disguise her usual expression of chronic bad temper.

"Who held a party in the haunted house?" she growled.

"We don't know! Tell us!" screamed the crowd.

"Who d'you think?" snarled Ratsnappy— "The ghostess. Here's another. What d'you say to a two-headed monster? Hallo hallo."

"Hear that? Hallo hallo! Get it? Oh ha ha ha!" roared the audience.

Ratsnappy, who only knew two jokes, signaled to the band to begin playing so that she could do the Funny Dance she had worked out. Sadly, she had only finished making her long clown shoes that morning, and hadn't actually practiced dancing in them. She only managed to do three hops and a twirl before falling flat on her face. She was carried off unconscious. The audience, convinced this was all part of the act, gave her a standing ovation.

Scrofula came next, sitting on a stool with her hand in a holey sock.

"Gottle of geer, gottle of geer," ground out Scrofula through gritted teeth, and waggled her fingers a bit, to make the sock look like it was talking.

"Hello, everygoggy, gy game ish Fred." (Get that?)

"Saw your lips move," shouted one of the Banshees.

"Gno you giggen." (No you didn't.)

"Yes we did." (Yes we did.)

"Gno you giggen!" (No you didn't!)

"Yes we did!" (Yes we did!)

"Giggen! Giggen!" (Didn't! Didn't!)

"Gig! Gig!" (Did! Did!)

It was all great fun, and everyone was disappointed when Scrofula wiggled her fingers just that bit too hard and the sock fell apart. No more sock, no more act—but everyone agreed that it had been wonderful while it lasted, and Scrofula took bow after triumphant bow.

Time now for Sludgegooey's Impressions. These proved enormously popular, because the impressions were all of her fellow Witches. She did Sharkadder making-up, Pongwiffy scenting a rubbish dump, Bonidle getting up in the morning, and Gaga trying to add up a milk bill. She never got any further than that, because Sharkadder, Pongwiffy, Bonidle and Gaga marched on stage looking very put out and bundled her off, much to the displeasure of the audience, who had loved it so far and wanted to see the rest. At this point, Scott Sinister woke up, checked his program, and was relieved to see that there were only two acts to go.

Sharkadder's Make-up Demonstration was next. The curtains parted, revealing a large table set out with mirrors, dozens of little pots, lipsticks, brushes, jars, combs and hair grips. Beneath the table was a huge bucket full of hot mud. Sharkadder, wearing orange ribbons, a shocking pink evening gown and so much rouge that it hurt to look at her, waltzed to the front of the stage and asked for a volunteer.

The audience with one accord shrank into their seats. Some went so far as to get down on hands and knees pretending they'd dropped their programs, so anxious were they not to volunteer. In the wings, Pongwiffy sniggered. Sharkadder heard.

"I thought of demonstrating on Pongwiffy," Sharkadder told the audience maliciously. "But there really doesn't seem much point. It would be like putting a fresh coat of paint on a very old and cracked wall. So perhaps . . ." she added sweetly. "Perhaps our distinguished guest would oblige. Up you come, Mr. Sinister!"

Scott Sinister was too much of a showman to refuse. With a tolerant smile he stood, graciously acknowledged the cheers of the audience and made his way to the stage, sinking elegantly into the chair Sharkadder had set ready. He glanced into the wings and suddenly began to get a bit worried by the sight of Pongwiffy shaking her head and mouthing "No! No!" with a desperate expression on her face.

"Look, I really don't think . . ." said Scott Sinister, attempting to rise.

"Too late, Mr. Sinister, you're mine now," trilled Sharkadder gaily, giving him a rough push and draping a towel around his neck. "Now, everybody, pay close attention, for I am about to demonstrate deep cleansing. For this, I use hot mud." And she scooped a large handful from the bucket and slapped it on Scott Sinister's face. It wasn't a pleasant experience. Firstly, it was uncomfortably hot, and secondly, a great deal of it went into his mouth.

"Groooougghch!" spluttered Scott Sinister. "Get . . . it . . . off!"

"Patience, Mr. Sinister," sang Sharkadder brightly. "We must wait a moment and let the cooling mudpack do its work, drawing out all the little impurities and hidden gunk that you never knew you had. Right, that should be long enough. Now, everybody, you will observe that I take this old rag and wipe it off, leaving a beautifully radiant skin, glowing with cleanliness."

And Sharkadder attempted to wipe off the mud. And this is the point at which she came unstuck.

And the reason she became unstuck is that the mud didn't. It didn't seem to want to shift at all. It remained firmly welded in a great glob to the famous Sinister's face.

And the reason that it wouldn't wipe off is because, unbeknown to Sharkadder, Pongwiffy had dropped in just a few drops of Stickee Kwickee

Superglue, the advertising slogan of which is "Falling apart? Gum and stick with us."

It was lethal stuff, instant and long lasting, and it was very wrong of Pongwiffy to have put it in Sharkadder's cleansing mud. Shall we throw her out of this story? What excuses does she have?

Well, of course, she has had a great deal of provocation since the affair of the missing hair rollers, which she genuinely hadn't taken. In fact, the hedgehogs had roused themselves enough one night to crawl off home by themselves. Shark-adder had accused Pongwiffy of stealing them, and written *PONGWIFFY IS A THEEF* in lipstick on tree trunks all over the forest, which was of course untrue.

So, although Pongwiffy has behaved very badly and had no right to spoil Sharkadder's chance of winning the Hugo award by playing such an underhand trick, perhaps we'll let her off. Particularly as the trick has misfired so badly and her beloved Scott is now thickly coated in a mudpack which has gone from globby to rock hard in seconds.

"Mmmmph!" wailed Scott Sinister, from somewhere underneath.

"Keep calm, Mr. Sinister. Can you hear me in there? I'm rubbing as hard as I can . . . It's funny, I can't get it off my hand either . . ." cried poor Sharkadder, who still hadn't twigged what had happened.

"Oh no! Oh no!" moaned Pongwiffy in the wings, rocking to and fro in horror as her idol flung himself from the chair and began to flail blindly about the stage, muttering, "grooo" and "blurk" and other muffled things like that. Pongwiffy had made the bad mistake, you see, of assuming that as usual Sharkadder would fail to get a volunteer and end up demonstrating on herself.

In the process of rocking, Pongwiffy's hat fell off, which was a pity because that was where she had hidden the tube of Stickee Kwickee after carrying out the evil deed.

"Aha!" screamed Sharkadder, seeing it fall. "Now I get it!" And all hell broke loose. Sharkadder scooped up a handful of mud and hurled it at Pongwiffy. It caught her slap in the left eye. Pongwiffy screeched and threw herself on Sharkadder. They rolled around the stage, tipping over the bucket of mud. It glopped all over

the place. Huge cheers came from the audience.

Scott Sinister, still staggering around, slipped as the hot tide lapped around his ankles and fell (you've got it) into the orchestra pit, putting his foot through Filth's one remaining drum and splattering the audience with glue-spiked mud.

Of course, the audience retaliated with ice cream, programs, benches and anything they could lay their hands on. Macabre came gallop-

ing back down the aisle on her Haggis, thinking it was straightforward mud wrestling. Witches and Familiars poured from backstage and waded in with a will. Within seconds the hall was in total uproar.

To crown it all, poor old Grandwitch Sourmuddle was standing on Sharkadder's table wearing a yellow party frock and singing *Happy birthday to me*, which of course was the surprise song which she hadn't had the chance to sing. (You'd guessed that, hadn't you?) Nobody noticed, which was rather sad. After all, she was very old and Mistress of the Coven.

And that was the end of the Great Talent Contest, if not the end of the evening. The end of the evening was a disgrace to all concerned, and we won't bother to describe it.

Several days later, Pongwiffy, still very sore from the special solvent she had used to remove the congealed mud from her left eye, legs and, I'm afraid, bottom, lay in her sickbed and stared sadly at the second letter from Scott Sinister. What it said doesn't bear repeating.

"I don't think I'll have it framed," she said sadly.

"I vouldn't," agreed Hugo.

"It's such a pity it ended like that. Nobody got

your Hugo Award. And he'll never speak to me again. When they chipped it off, one of his fangs came out, you know. Oh Scott, Scott. It's all my fault." And Pongwiffy burst into tears.

"Cheer up, Mistress," said Hugo. " 'Ere. For you." He handed Pongwiffy a little box. In it was the Hugo Award.

"Oh, thanks, Hugo," said Pongwiffy, pleased. "You're a good little chap. By the way, did you take that solvent around to Sharky?"

"Ya, but she von't use it. She say she vait and get her own. Still she not speak to you."

"Talk about bearing a grudge. Two days later, and she still hasn't forgiven me. You know what she is?"

"Vat?"

"Stuck-up," said Pongwiffy. Which was true.

CHAPTER EIGHT

PREPARATIONS

Sourmuddle's two hundredth birthday was only a week away. Sourmuddle seemed to have forgotten all about it, which was a funny thing considering that's all she ever seemed to talk about. It was probably because she had been wrong about the date so many times she had given up hope of it ever arriving.

The Witches were determined that her party was going to be a Really Good Do. It was an important occasion, not just because reaching two hundred deserves celebration, but because Sourmuddle had often hinted that she intended to retire at two hundred, which meant she would have to name her successor as Mistress of the Coven.

All the Witches fancied the job, because of the perks. These included: unlimited credit at Malpractice Magic Ltd., the shop where the Witches bought all their equipment; a new Broom with a year's free service, including a complete bristle change and respray; a rather desirable two-up-two-down cottage in a better part of the wood; three weeks' paid holiday; trial offers of every new magic powder that came on the market and an annual invitation to the Wizard's Ball. Best of all, you could boss everyone around, which was the real reason why everyone wanted the job.

Grandwitch Sourmuddle had noticed that everyone was avoiding her. Wherever she went, Witches were whispering and going into huddles. All this talking behind her back worried her so much that she became convinced that everyone was plotting a mutiny against her. She got so nervous about it, she confiscated all Wands, claiming that she wanted to check them for Wand rot. At least the enemy was now deprived of their main weapons. She then barricaded herself into her cottage and set about weaving complicated spells designed to protect herself when the revolution came. This was good, because it meant the Witches were free to get to work planning her surprise party.

There was a lot of quareling as usual, because all of them wanted to be seen doing the most important job, which would be another point in their favor when Sourmuddle decided who should step into her boots as Grandwitch.

The thing that caused the most argument was The Cake. After all, apart from cards and presents it's The Cake that makes a birthday seem like a birthday. Each Witch was convinced that she was the best cook for miles around, and wanted the glory of making Sourmuddle's cake. The row was really beginning to get out of hand when Sharkadder put an end to it by suggesting that the fairest thing would be to have a collection and buy one, and that she would have a word with Pierre de Gingerbeard, the famous chef, who just happened to be her cousin.

This commanded a respectful silence. Everybody had heard of the great Pierre de Gingerbeard, author of *Buttered Snails and Other Tales*. Why, even the Wizards begged him to cook for their banquets! Fancy Sharkadder being related to him. Even Pongwiffy was impressed, and glad that she and Sharkadder were best friends. Yes, they were friends again. Pongwiffy unraveled one of her old cardigans and knitted Dudley a blanket for his cat basket. He refused to use it, but the thought was there, and Sharkadder's heart had melted in no time.

"So it's decided, then," said Sharkadder. "I'll go and order it tomorrow. You can come with me, Pong."

"Oh thanks, Sharky," beamed Pongwiffy. "I'd like that." After all, helping order The Cake was an important job.

So the final list was drawn up of who should be responsible for what. It went like this:

Agglebag and Bagaggle — Music
Bendyshanks and Bonidle — Decorashuns
Gaga — Crackers, Crazy Hats
Greymatter and Macable — Games
Ratsnappy, Scrofula and Sludgegooey — Food
Sharkadder and Pongwiffy — The kake

And everyone was happy. Until the collection hat came around, that is. But then, you'd expect that, wouldn't you?

"Ooo? Ooo deed you say you are?" The ancient, barrel-shaped Dwarf with the tall white hat and the famous curling ginger beard peered at them with suspicious little curranty eyes. He sat at a small table in the middle of the great Gingerbeard Kitchens, stumpy little fingers nimbly molding green marzipan frogs which he carefully placed in fancy boxes. They were so lifelike, those frogs, you could almost imagine them leaping out of their little paper nests and straight into your mouth.

"Sharkadder, Cousin Pierre," explained Sharkadder for the third time. "I used to sit on your knee. At family get-togethers."

"Seet on my knee? You? Ees a joke, oui?"

"Well, of course, I was little at the time. Look, surely you remember . . ."

Pongwiffy shuffled and whistled a little tune. The truth is, she was embarrassed. Early that morning, she and Sharkadder had set off for the Ginger-beard Kitchens. That's the name given to those huge caverns lying deep in the heart of the Misty Mountains where Pierre de Gingerbeard, famous chef, rules O.K.

It was a long climb, not made easier by the fact that they had to carry their Broomsticks, daytime flying being strictly forbidden. As they had puffed up the steep slope, Pongwiffy had gaily prattled on to Sharkadder about how wonderful it was that Sharkadder was related to the famous chef, and why hadn't she mentioned it before, it wasn't like her to be so modest, etc., etc.

Sharkadder had got quieter and quieter, and finally confessed that actually, they weren't *that* closely related. Pongwiffy remarked that cousins were quite close. Sharkadder said it depended on how many times removed. Pongwiffy asked how many times removed. Sharkadder said she'd for-gotten, but a few times. Pongwiffy pressed for the exact number of times. Sharkadder said twenty-four, actually, but she always sent him a Christmas card, and she was sure he'd remember her. Pongwiffy announced that she wanted to go home. Sharkadder sulked. Pongwiffy sulked harder. Sharkadder went all sad and finally burst into tears, so in the end Pongwiffy had agreed to accompany her, more, it must be confessed, because of the wonderful smell of baking wafting down the mountain, than any thoughts of loyalty or friendship.

So there they were in the famous Gingerbeard Kitchens. Everywhere was hustle and bustle, with sweating Dwarfs stoking the great ovens into which went huge trays of pies, tarts, loaves, and cakes. More Dwarfs scurried to and fro with trays of eclairs, doughnuts and cherry slices balanced on their heads. Massive vats of chocolate bubbled and boiled, stirred and fussed over by the chocolate chefs; pastry chefs were pummeling dough with huge red hands; buckets of thick, rich cream were lined up half submerged in troughs of cool water; sacks of flour and sugar were being heaved about; and shelves groaned under the weight of big pots of jam. The air was redolent with the most wonderful, warm, sugary, slavery baking smell. Pongwiffy sniffed and drooled, desperately hoping that Pierre de Gingerbeard might offer them a few samples. But he hadn't so far.

"You see, my mother's aunty was your father's nephew's niece's fifth cousin twice removed on my granny's side . . ." Sharkadder was explaining again, wriggling uncomfortably as the skeptical little currant eyes bore into her.

"We are rrrelated? You are a cuzain of mine?"

"Yes. Isn't it fun?" said Sharkadder with a merry little laugh.

"So," grunted Pierre de Gingerbeard, continuing to mold the marzipan frogs. He was obviously a genius. Not only was he able to create tiny miracles with his thick, stubby fingers, he had the right sort of accent.

"So. We are rrrrelated. We are cuzains, twenty-fourrr times rrremoved. And you must be zat nasty leetle weetch keed 'oo used to pull my beard. Ze one 'oo sends me cheap Chreestmas carrrds and drops 'ints about 'ow much you would like a free puddeeeng. Oui?"

"Mmmmm," said Sharkadder uncomfortably, with a sideways look at Pongwiffy.

"Hum. Well, Cuzain Sharkaddaire. To what do I owe ze honaire of zees veesit? You are steel 'oping for a puddeeeeng? Or 'ave you come to sponge a sponge, huh?"

"No, not a sponge," began Pongwiffy.

Sharkadder interrupted. "Sssh, Pong. He's my relative. No, not a sponge, Cousin Gingerbeard. A Cake. A Very Special Cake, actually. And we've got the money to pay for it. It's for Grandwitch Sourmuddle, you see. It's her two-hundredth birthday soon, and she's going to retire. We hope."

"A two-hundredth birthday cake, you say?" Pierre de Gingerbeard looked thoughtful. "Now, one of zose I 'ave not made een yearrrs. 'Ow beeg you want zees cake?"

"Oh, big. Ever so big. It's got to be special, you see."

"Uh, huh. A beeg, reech fruit cake, oui? Weez thick yellow marzipan and snowy white iceeng, decorrated weez leetle weetch 'ats, and a beeg pink ribbon, and candles and beautiful writing saying 'appy birthday, oui?"

"That's what we had in mind, yes."

Pierre de Gingerbeard closed his eyes and seemed to go into a trance. Pongwiffy just had time to snatch a box of frogs and a couple of doughnuts from a passing tray and shove them under her hat before his eyes snapped open again.

"Such a cake only Pierre de Gingerbeard can

make," roared the genius, fists clenched above his head. "I weel crreate zees cake for you, Cuzain Sharkaddaire, not because you are my cuzain twenty-four times rremoved, but because I adore to make two-hundredth birthday cakes, and I don't get ze chance often. Zees cake, Cuzain Sharkaddaire . . ." he paused for effect. "Zees Cake Weel Be My Mastairepiece!"

A week later, and the day before Sourmuddle's party, Pongwiffy and Sharkadder were again in the Gingerbeard Kitchens, staring in awed wonder as Pierre de Gingerbeard unveiled the masterpiece.

"Voila!" said Pierre de Gingerbeard. "Get ze load of zat, zen!"

Pongwiffy and Sharkadder gaped at the creation, and broke into spontaneous applause. It was wonderful. It stood in all its glory on a silver platter, big as a dustbin lid, mouthwateringly magnificent, truly the Cake of All Cakes.

Think of that cake you once saw in a baker's window, the one you drooled over for hours before being dragged off home and made to eat your cauliflower. Now forget it. Compared to Sourmuddle's Cake, that cake of your dreams is the sort of thing you could whip up out of a packet in half an hour.

The icing alone on this Cake would put the snowy wastes of Greenland to shame, so dazzling was its whiteness. The sides were decorated with fine trelliswork with never a drip, blob or wobble. Two hundred little sugar broomsticks were positioned around the edge, and two hundred small black candles were placed cleverly on the top, surrounding the piped words, *HAPPY BIRTHDAY SOURMUDDLE, TWO HUNDRED GLORIOUS YEARS*. Two hundred tiny witch hats had been cunningly fitted on as well, and a huge pink bow added the final touch. What a cake!

"Wow!" breathed Pongwiffy and Sharkadder together. "Wow."

"Eet ees, as you say, wow," agreed Pierre de

Gingerbeard, wiping away tears of emotion. "Ees work of art."

"Cousin Gingerbeard, you're a genius," crowed Sharkadder. "There's only one thing that bothers me."

"I know what you're going to say, Sharky," agreed Pongwiffy. "How are we going to get it home?"

"No. How much discount do I get? Seeing I'm family?"

In the finish, they got it home by Magic. Struggling down the mountain with the huge Cake was a daunting prospect, as the sun was setting and shortly it would be dark. It was too big to balance on a Broomstick, so that was out.

Delivery seemed out of the question, as immediately after Sharkadder's query about discount, Pierre de Gingerbeard had passed out. Probably sheer creative exhaustion. Anyway, right now he was being carted off to bed on the only stretcher large enough to bear The Cake. It would seem rather ungrateful to insist that he be tipped off.

Magic had to be the answer. The trouble was, their Wands had been confiscated. They both racked their brains for an old spell which didn't need one in order to work. Pongwiffy, after much thought, finally came up with an ancient, dimly remembered, Spell of Transport.

"Are you sure it'll work?" said Sharkadder dubiously. "I don't trust those old spells. Unreliable. And are you sure you can get it right?"

"Positive. I learned it at school. You never forget what you learn at school. Now, where do we want to keep The Cake?"

"I don't know. Somewhere safe. We don't want anyone to see it before tomorrow night, else it'll spoil the surprise."

"What about my garden shed?" suggested Pongwiffy. "It's got a big padlock, and no one'll think of looking there. And I'll be nearby to guard it."

You didn't know Pongwiffy had a garden

shed, did you? Well, she does. She uses it to grow toadstools from seed, and sometimes locks the Broom in it when it gets on her nerves.

"Hmm. All right," agreed Sharkadder. "You're sure it'll be safe?"

"I'm sure. Right, here goes. How did that spell go again? Oh yes, I remember . . ."

"Look, if your spell harms so much as one crumb of that Cake . . ." threatened Sharkadder.

"It won't, it won't. I know it now. Listen, you might learn something."

"Hey! Look at that, it's working. See? I told you."

Sure enough, The Cake rose several inches off the ground, wobbled a bit, then, very slowly and jerkily, gained in height until it was on a level with the treetops. Pongwiffy and Sharkadder watched it, squinting their eyes against the setting sun.

"It's slow all right, I'll grant you that," said Sharkadder, pulling worriedly at her nose. "I'm not so sure about steady, though."

"It'll get there," said Pongwiffy, watching The Cake lose height, gain it, lose it again, wobble off in totally the wrong direction, wobble back again, hesitate, narrowly avoid a head-on collision with a surprised eagle, dither uncertainly, then finally drift off to vanish behind a peak. "I think."

CHAPTER NINE

THIEVES

Now, this happened on a Tuesday. Remember the significant thing about Tuesday? It's the *Goblin's Hunting Night!* They were plodding back to their cave, trying hard to look forward to their supper, which was last night's warmed-up salt-flavored water because, as usual, they hadn't succeeded in catching anything.

Well, let's be fair and give credit where it's due. Young Sproggit, at great risk to himself, had at one point made a flying tackle and brought a small glowworm to its knees. But they all agreed that it was too small to divide satisfactorily into seven bits, and wasn't worth the trouble of carrying all the way home. So Sproggit let it go again.

Apart from that brief drama, the hunt had followed its usual pattern of checking empty traps, crashing around and bumping into trees, losing each other, falling into swamps and ditches, trying to talk like carrots in case rabbits were listening, and holding their hunting bags wide open in the hopes that something might jump in. Nothing did, of course. It never does. You'd think they'd learn.

They were so fed up, they almost started fighting then and there—but agreed that perhaps they should wait until they got home, otherwise there would be nothing to do until they drank the warmed-up, salt-flavored water at midnight—traditionally the Goblin's supper time. It was a silly Tradition, as they were always starving long before then—but all Goblin Traditions are silly, as we know. Of course, nobody thought of moving supper time forward by an hour or so. That's Goblins for you.

Anyway. Home, the Goblins were trudging, sulky and defeated, not even bothering to sing. Most had their bobble hats firmly pulled down over their faces as protection against bumping into trees. They couldn't see the trees, of course, because their hats were over their faces.

One, however, was hatless, having caught a loose thread on an overhanging branch the minute he had left the cave that evening. The hat had gradually unraveled during the course of the hunt, and although his brains seemed a little chillier than usual, he noticed nothing particularly out of the ordinary until somebody pointed out his bare head and the line of wool trailing all over the wood, tying up the trees in a sort of gigantic, tangled cat's cradle.

The bareheaded Goblin was looking up at the moon, wondering if it was indeed made of cheese, and if so, was it the ripe, round, smelly sort or the kind that comes in thin slices? It couldn't be the sort that came in little triangles, for the shape was all wrong. Though, come to think of it, so is the shape of the thin slices . . .

You will gather from this that the hatless Goblin who was looking up at the moon was incredibly stupid. He was also incredibly big. Got it? Yes, it was our old friend, Plugugly, and because he leads such a dull life with those brains of his, it seems only fair to let him be the first to spot the flying Cake.

"Derrrrrr . . ." he croaked, eyes bulging, nudging everyone furiously and pointing upward. "Will you look at dat! Dat's a flying cup, dat is!"

"Saucer, you mean," said young Sproggit cockily. "The saucer's what goes under the cup, see, to catch the drips. The cup's what you drink out of."

"Yer?" said Plugugly wonderingly. " 'Sfunny, I always do it the uvver way around."

Silence fell as the Goblins watched The Cake. It was acting rather strangely, zigzagging across the sky, plummeting down, zooming up high, obviously unsure of where it was going.

" 'Snorra saucer, anyway," remarked Hog, adding wisely, "You kin tell. Too fat fer a saucer."

"He's right," agreed Slopbucket. "But if iss-norra saucer, warrisit?"

"Issa U.F.O., dat's what," said Eyesore.

"Wassat?"

"I dunno, do I? Unattractive Female Ostrich?"

"Nah, 'Snorra *nostrich*. Can't fly, kin they?"

"You got any better ideas den?"

"Yer, issa spaceship, dat's worritiz. 'N iss gonna land, an' norrible ugly little green fings is gonna come out and take over de world!"

"Per'aps we'd better run fer it, den."

"Nah. 'Old yer ground. Can't be uglier than us, kin they?"

The Cake was hovering directly over their heads. They watched it a moment longer, then Plugugly cleared his throat. "Know what I fink dat is? I fink dat's A Cake. An' if issa Cake, I fink we should foller it an' see where it lands, an' den . . . an' den steal it, yer, steal it, an' den . . . an' den . . ." Plugugly's brains got in a knot at that point, but the Goblins caught his drift.

"Yer! Eat it! Her her her, eat it! Hooray!" they yelled, throwing their hats in the air and kicking each other excitedly. Above them, The Cake suddenly remembered where it was going and floated off again, so the Goblins hastily got into hunting formation and tiptoed after it with much uncouth bellowing and disgustingly greedy howls.

Now, if you remember, Pongwiffy's Spell of Transport ordered the air currents to take The Cake to her garden shed. It was an old, creaky, inefficient sort of spell which is hardly ever used these days. Wands are so much better, in the way that calculators are generally more fast and reliable than sums worked out in yellow crayon on the back of an old envelope.

The Magic controlling the air currents was primitive Magic, the sort of Magic that couldn't really cope with unexpected circumstances. Like the shed being locked.

These unreliable air currents, having taken The Cake around the air equivalent of winding country lanes instead of straight as the crow flies,

finally got it to Pongwiffy's shed. The large padlock on the door was a major technical hitch, and
they had no idea how to cope with it. They there-
fore simply deposited their burden gently in
Pongwiffy's prize nettle patch and blew away,
eager to get back and play amongst the pine trees
on the mountain.

All would have been well if Pongwiffy had
come straight home. She would most probably
have arrived before The Cake, and the shed
would have been unlocked and everything would
have been hunky dory. However, it didn't happen
that way.

Halfway home, she suffered a rather unpleas-
ant attack of air sickness (brought on, no doubt, by
too many marzipan frogs and stolen doughnuts)
and had to order the Broom to make an emer-
gency landing on a village green. There, she drank
a great deal of water from the pump, and lay
around moaning feebly and holding her stomach
while the Broom idled around and struck up a
conversation with a nearby lawn mower.

Sharkadder, who had also pinched some
marzipan frogs but had the willpower to save
them for later, flew straight home, lulled into a
false sense of security by Pongwiffy's assurances
that the spell would work and that anyway, she

(Pongwiffy) would definitely arrive back before The Cake did, and would make absolutely sure it was safely settled down for the night, so no worries, no problems, etc., etc.

Of course, Sharkadder should have worried. If, instead of climbing into her dressing gown and slapping on several layers of bedtime cleansing mud, she had gone to check that both The Cake and Pongwiffy had arrived back, The Cake would never have been stolen by Goblins.

But she didn't. So it was.

"I beg your pardon? For one moment there, I thought you said The Cake had been stolen, ha ha ha," said Sharkadder, standing at the door in her nightcap, face crisp with dried cleansing mud, chin flaked with green marzipan, clutching a mug of Awfultine, obviously just about to get into bed.

"I did! It has been! I came right over, Sharky, quick as I could," babbled poor Pongwiffy. "It wasn't my fault," she added.

"Stolen? You mean . . . *stolen?*" said Sharkadder stupidly, unable to take it in.

"Yes! Yes! By Goblins!"

"Goblins? If this is a joke . . ."

"No! No joke. It's true."

"Goblins have stolen The Cake? Sourmuddle's

Birthday Cake? *Cousin Gingerbeard's Masterpiece?*"

"Yes, I keep *saying.* I know it was Goblins, because I've got evidence. Look!" Pongwiffy thrust a filthy bobbly hat under Sharkadder's nose.

"See? One of them must have dropped it. The Cake got back all right, my nettle patch is full of icing sugar crumbs. But it couldn't get into the shed because of the padlock. So the Goblins must have seen it sitting there in the garden. We're lucky they didn't eat it on the spot, but I know they didn't because there's this trail of crumbs leading to their cave. Besides, they never eat out. So they must have it in there, and they'll start eating it on the first stroke of midnight. That's their supper time. Oh, Sharky, what are we going to do?"

Sharkadder decided then and there what she was going to do. Without any hesitation, she

fainted clean away, right there on the doorstep. It wasn't much help.

Pongwiffy debated whether to revive her, and decided against it. When Sharkadder came around she would doubtless start shouting and saying I-told-you-so and breaking friends and things like that. Best to leave her there and try to get The Cake back by herself. How, badness only knew— but try she would. After all, one Witch, even without her Wand, is more than a match for a Gaggle of Goblins. Especially if that Witch is our Pong.

The Goblins, meanwhile, could hardly believe their luck. After weeks of coming home with nothing more than severe headaches, they had at last succeeded in tracking down and capturing An Entire Cake. What's more, it was a Witch's Birthday Cake! The Goblins couldn't read the writing on the top, but the icing sugar Broomsticks and Witch hats were clues which even they could understand. There were a lot of candles, too, which meant that the birthday Witch was probably quite old. The Goblins could only count up to ten, but all agreed that there were lots more than that.

Lardo suggested that perhaps it was that ol' Pongwiffy's Birthday Cake, as it had been captured whilst sitting in her front garden. This made them even more gleeful. What a laugh, to eat that 'ol Pongwiffy's Birthday Cake—wouldn't she be furious, har har har.

All this jollity passed the time rather pleasantly, until it was five minutes to midnight. They were sitting in a circle on the floor, surrounding the wonderful Cake which was set on a low barrel at the cave center. Sproggit, the official time-keeper, being the only one with a watch, commenced the countdown. This was a particularly pointless Tradition, as his watch only told the time in days and both the hands were missing. It wasn't necessary anyway, as Goblins always know when it's midnight because their empty stomachs begin to itch. They call it the Itching Hour.

Anyway, Sproggit was doing the countdown, Slopbucket was sharpening the cake knife, and the air was filled with the horrible drooling, slobbering, lipsmacking, stomach scratching sounds which precede every Goblin meal.

"Fifty-nine seconds . . ." intoned Sproggit. "Fifty-ten seconds . . . er . . . forty-twelve . . ."

And then it happened. Of all inconvenient things, there came a brisk knocking at the front door—or front boulder, if you want to be fussy.

The Goblins looked at each other in alarm. Supposing it was that old Pongwiffy, come to claim back The Cake? They hissed and gibbered fearfully as Plugugly went to answer the boulder, which was *his* official job.

When he came back again, he wasn't alone. With him was a Mysterious Stranger, wearing clothing that was rather Spanish in style and carrying a wicker basket containing bunches of heather. She looked very exotic.

Around her head was tied a spotted headscarf. She wore a blouse with big puffy sleeves, a purple shawl, a swirly red skirt and lots of jangling jewelry including huge hoop earrings and a pendant in the shape of a crystal ball. She also wore a large pair of sunglasses, which added to the air of mystery.

We know who it is, don't we? We're not stupid like the Goblins. We'd know Pongwiffy anywhere, if only by her smell. Mind you, she had done rather a good job with her disguise. The only thing which rather spoilt the overall effect was her boots, but that wasn't her fault. When she tried taking them off, Hugo had insisted she put them back on again *immediately.* So the disguise isn't perfect in every detail. But if you ever caught a whiff of Pongwiffy's exposed feet, you too would feel it was a risk worth taking.

"Good evening, kind sirs!" trilled Pongwiffy, rattling a pair of castinets. "Buy a few pegs from the gypsy woman. Fortunes told, cross my palm with silver, Flamenco dancing a specialty, get your lucky heather here!"

"Says she's a fortune-teller," growled Plugugly with a jerk of his thumb.

"Indeed I am. A poor gypsy fortune-teller, that's me. I tell the best fortune for miles around, I do."

"It'd better be short," said Plugugly. "Cos we're 'avin' our supper."

"So I see, sir, so I see. And what a lovely Cake that is, sir."

"Never mind that. Warrabout my fortune?"

"Patience, sir, patience. Don't want to bring the Gypsy Curse down upon your head do you? Oh, but what a lucky face you have, sir! See that wart, right there on your nose? That means a journey, sir, a long journey over water. And that pimple on your neck stands for a tall stranger who will bring you good luck."

"Yer? Gerraway!" said Plugugly, pleased.

"Now, let me see your hand." Pongwiffy causally placed her basket on the floor and inspected Plugugly's filthy paw, bracelets jangling.

"Aha. I thought so. It's all here, you know. Plain as can be. You're going to meet a beautiful She-Goblin with long matted hair like old rope and little red piggy eyes. She'll fall in love with you at first sight."

"Cor. Just my type. 'Ear that, you lot?"

"And what's more, I see a wedding, with much dancing and delicious things to eat. And what's this? Oho! Oh ho ho ho! I see six—no, seven little baby Goblins, bald they are, climbing all over you, sir, and calling you daddy."

"Yer? You can really see all that?" said Plugugly, his eyes misting over.

"Clear as day. It's all here, on your love line. In fact, one's being sick down your shirt right now."

Pongwiffy's performance was going down rather well, much to her relief. The other Goblins in the cave had torn their piggy eyes away from The Cake, and were listening intently, mouths open.

"And their names," continued Pongwiffy, "their names are written here as well. Skwawk, Shreek, Grizzle, Boo, Hoo, and er—Plop." That only came to six, of course, but the Goblins didn't notice, so it didn't matter.

"My little boys," wept Plugugly emotionally. "What lovely names!"

"They're girls actually," Pongwiffy corrected him. "Except for Plop."

"Even better. I'll buy six pink frilly dresses ter go wiv dere bovver boots. An' a blue Goblin-gro fer Plop."

By now, the Goblins were all beginning to crowd around, eager to hear the rest of Plugugly's fortune and dying to have their own hands read. So intent were they at being first in the queue, they didn't notice the small Hamster, disguised as a bunch of heather, slip out of the basket, scuttle toward The Cake, swing himself up and tuck himself out of sight in the folds of the pink bow.

"What else, gypsy?" Plugugly was saying. "Anyfin' else?"

"That's all I see on your love line. Now, let's look at your life line, shall we? Wait a minute. Where is it? You haven't got one!"

"Eh?"

"I don't believe it, everyone has a life line—ah, here it is. But it's so short! I've never seen one as short as this. According to this line, your life is about to end very, very soon."

"What? How soon?" Plugugly had gone very white, and his hand trembled.

"According to this, in about five minutes."

"What? 'Ang on, you muster made a mistake."

"Oh sir, sir, the lines don't lie! There's going to be a dreadful catastrophe. It's written quite plainly on your palm. Hold your hands up, everyone, quick! Yes, yes, it's as I thought! You've all got short life lines! There's going to be a disaster. Oh, doom, doom. Doom and woe!"

"What? What's going to happen?" quavered the alarmed Goblins.

"What about my little girls?" wailed Plugugly. "And Plop? What about Plop?"

"Yes, it's very unfortunate, I do agree," said Pongwiffy, shaking her head with a worried look. "But disaster's at hand, I feel sure of that. The question is, what sort of disaster? Flood? Fire? Plague? Maddened Pandas? Killer Ladybirds? Blood Crazed Bunny Rabbits? Could be anything, hard to say. Of course, the most likely thing is a bomb."

"What did she say? A what?" gibbered the Goblins, eyes bulging.

"A bomb. I've just got this feeling that there's a bomb somewhere in this cave, and any minute now it's going to go off! We have to find it, there's not a minute to lose! Think, kind sirs, think, I beg of you! Has anything been brought into this cave recently which is . . . *big enough to hide a bomb?*"

Pongwiffy stared pointedly at The Cake, but the Goblins merely shrugged, looked frightened and gnawed their fingernails. The word Bomb had clearly sent them into a state of shock, and their brains had jammed. She saw she would have to spell it out even more clearly.

"Now, let's not panic. We must remain calm. We are looking for a bomb. A bomb in disguise, a cleverly hidden bomb. Now, what do bombs do? Think!"

The Goblins looked blank. Bombs, bombs. What did bombs do again? They knew it was something awful, it was on the tip of their tongues but they just couldn't think . . .

"Why, they tick, of course! Let's all be very quiet for a moment, and see if we can hear ticking." There was an instant silence. Then:

"Teek," went The Cake, dead on cue. "Teek, teek, teek, teek . . ."

"That cake!" howled Pongwiffy, pointing a trembling finger. "There's a bomb in The Cake! It's going to go off!"

That was it! That's what bombs do! They go off! Seven Goblin mouths opened and let out seven Goblin howls. And before you could say bobblehat, the cave was deserted!

"You see? Told you it'd work," said Pongwiffy to Hugo as the screaming faded away in the distance. "Nothing to it. Operation Cake Rescue successful. At ease, Sergeant."

"Not quite," said Hugo, emerging from his hiding place and pulling heather from his ears. "Vee 'asn't got it 'ome yet."

"Elementary, my dear Hugo. I shall use a Rolling Spell. I don't trust that Spell of Transport."

"A Rollink Spell?"

"Yes, I learnt it in school. How did it go again? Oh yes, I know. Stand back Hugo, how often do I have to tell you I need room when I cast spells? Right.

> *Rolling drums and rolling pins*
>
> *Rolls of fat make double chins,*
>
> *Rock and roll is here to stay,*
>
> *Make this Cake now roll away!*

And after a moment, to their great relief, The Cake heaved, shuddered, shifted sideways, crawled off the silver platter and plopped on to the floor in a shower of crumbs. Several Witch hats and Broomsticks became unstuck in the process, but at least the spell was working. Once on the floor, it flipped over on its side and began to roll toward the cave's exit. Pongwiffy and Hugo scurried after it and emerged into the moonlit night just in time to see it go rolling briskly down the slope, looking rather like a giant runaway junior aspirin.

"Some of ze decorations, see, zey fall! Make it go slower," squeaked Hugo as they scrambled down after it, tripping over hidden roots and inconveniently placed boulders.

"Slower, Cake!" howled Pongwiffy, falling headlong over a tree stump and grazing her knees quite badly. "Oh bother, I've lost my scarf! I said, Slower, Cake!"

The Cake didn't seem to be slowing down at all. If anything, it was gaining speed. Before Pongwiffy had picked herself up, it had reached the bottom of the hill, and was already halfway-up another one.

"Ve 'ave to let it go," gasped Hugo, ringing sweat from his whiskers. "Ve never catch it now."

"Oh no? That's what you think!" Pongwiffy's voice took on that deep, important, ringing tone that actors always use when making an important speech. She clenched her fist in the air as well. All things considered, she really looked quite good. A pity her knee was bleeding, though.

"I shall follow this Cake wherever it leads!" she thundered. "Let no one stand in my way! However long it takes, however far the path may lead, even to the ends of the earth, I shall follow! The way may be long and hard, fraught with dangers and perils, but I shall follow! The rivers may be deep and the mountains high . . ."

There was a great deal more of the same, but that's enough for you to get the idea. And this

seems a rather good moment for us to leave. Let's move on to exactly twenty-four and a half hours later. We're allowed to do that if we want. We should spend a bit of time with Sourmuddle. After all, she is two hundred years old.

CHAPTER TEN

THE PARTY

Twenty-four and a half hours later, was the night of Grandwitch Sourmuddle's birthday party. Of course, Sourmuddle didn't know this. She thought it was just another monthly Crag Hill Sabbat meeting. She was, however, Expecting Trouble. The whispering and giggling behind her back had become more noticeable of late, and even Snoop was nowhere to be found. Sourmuddle was totally convinced that there was treachery in the air—but she wasn't Coven Mistress for nothing. She was prepared.

She zoomed in, dismounted, parked her Broomstick and marched into the glade. She was in full combat gear—armor-plated hat, spellproof vest, flak rags, the lot. She was also hung about with charms, amulets, talismans, bells, books and candles. She held a Wand in one hand a sawn-off pea shooter in the other. She bristled with stink bombs and wishbones. Her pockets were crammed with powders and philters of every description, and she was prepared, at a moment's notice, to vanish, turn into a leopard, shrink, grow into a giantess, or anything which

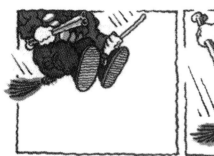 

might be appropriate, depending on what the rebel Witches chose to throw at her. In other words, she was Ready for Action. Plot against the Coven Mistress, would they? She'd show 'em.

The Witches and their Familiars were all assembled on the hill. There was no evidence of any weapons, Sourmuddle noticed. In fact, they seemed to be wearing party rags—but this was probably all part of the plan to pull the wool over her eyes.

"Right, you lot, do your worst!" shrilled Sourmuddle, taking up a battle pose and glaring around. "I know you've been plotting against me! I'm not stupid, you know. I'm not Grandwitch for nothing! Oh, so there you are, Snoop, you traitor. Gone over to the enemy, eh? Well, I don't need you. I don't need anyone. I . . . what are all these decorations doing?"

Suddenly, Sourmuddle became aware of the strings of gaily colored Witch lights strung through the trees. There were paper streamers too, and lanterns. And what was this? The trestle tables were literally groaning with delicious things to eat. Jellies, little sausages on sticks, cheese straws, chocolate biscuits, ice cream, more ice cream—and not a stale spiderspread sandwich in sight! There were crackers, too, and red serviettes!

And *what was that? A pile of . . . presents?*

"What's going on?" quavered Sourmuddle, confused. "What's hap . . ." But her voice was drowned out.

"Happy Birthday tooo yooooouuuu . . ." sang the Witches. *"Happy Birthday tooo yooooouuuu . . ."*

Sourmuddle couldn't believe her ears. Her *birthday?* At last, it was really her BIRTHDAY? And she had thought . . . all that whispering and huddling in corners . . . she had thought they . . .

"Oh," she whispered, a lump in her throat. "Oh. Thank you girls, I . . . I didn't know, you see, I . . ."

"We wanted it to be a surprise!" shouted the Witches, crowding around.

"Oh, it's that. It's that all right," bawled Sourmuddle, mopping her eyes, feeling an absolute idiot. That she could have mistrusted her own girls. That she could have thought even for one minute that . . . oh, what a fool she had been!

She wasn't allowed to stay miserable for long, however. Gaga passed around her homemade crazy hats, which were *really* crazy, and that was the signal for the festivities to start in earnest. First, Sourmuddle had to open all the cards, which was done rather hastily because she was dying to get on to the presents. And what presents!

There was a pair of bookends in the shape of Broomsticks from Agglebag and Bagaggle. They were a bit flimsy for bookends, being made of paper, but everyone agreed that they were very clever.

Bonidle's gift was a paperweight in the shape of an old brick. Well, to be honest, it *was* an old brick, but Bonidle had tied a red ribbon around it, so it looked quite pretty for a brick.

"What a lot of trouble you've gone to, Bonidle," said Sourmuddle happily, and Bonidle flushed with pride.

Gaga's present was a cardboard box containing some loose screws (she had plenty of those), some orange peel (fertilizer for Sourmuddle's tomato plants), an egg which ticked when shaken and which Gaga thought would hatch into a cuckoo clock, and some joke bat droppings. At least, Sourmuddle rather hoped that they *were* joke ones. At any rate, she said that she liked all the things, and couldn't wait for the cuckoo clock to hatch. Gaga was so pleased she had to rush off and hang upside down from a tree for a bit.

Macabre's tartan hanky was a great success. Sourmuddle tried it out right away, and didn't mind a bit when her nose immediately became a riot of small red and green squares, which didn't wash off for a fortnight—Macabre's uncle again, who also dealt in dyes.

"I like it," declared Sourmuddle, examining her tartan nose in a mirror. "I feel it's me. Thanks, Macabre."

Another triumph was Greymatter's book of crossword puzzles, which Greymatter had already thoughtfully filled in.

Ratsnappy's stinging nettle plant would look

just perfect on her coffee table, declared Sour-muddle. And the bottle of homemade shampoo from Scrofula was just what she needed, as her dandruff had recently shown alarming signs of going away.

Sludgegooey's sink plunger was duly admired, as was the set of lipsticks from Sharkadder in six shades of green: Moss, Nettle, Seaweed, Mold, Bile and Scummy Pond.

Sharkadder? Yes, you will be relieved to hear that Sharkadder had recovered from her fainting fit of the night before, and was there with the rest of them.

Only Pongwiffy was absent, and the truth was that nobody had even noticed in the excitement. Even if they had, it was unlikely that they would have cared that much, they were all having far too good a time.

We care, though, don't we? Perhaps we should leave the party and go and find her. On second thought, don't let's bother, for something rather interesting is about to happen.

The presents had all been unwrapped and Sourmuddle was sitting, glowing with pleasure, amidst the wrapping paper, examining all her new things. Sharkadder suddenly took command. She clapped her hands and called for silence.

"'Tea next!" she announced. There was a burst of clapping and loud cheers, and a surge toward the trestle tables.

"Hold it! First, a surprise. Are you ready back there?"

"Oui!" came a familiar voice from somewhere in the bushes. And from out of those bushes, you'll be astounded to hear, marched none other than Pierre de Gingerbeard—and in his wake came two more Dwarfs carrying between them a large stretcher on which was sitting:

THE CAKE!

A cry of wonder went up as the Witches saw The Cake for the first time. There it sat, a great snowy mountain, every Witch hat and Broomstick in place and pink bow crisply curled. The two hundred candles were alight, and it looked so beautiful, the Witches were awestruck—especially Sourmuddle, who burst into tears of gratitude. It was a moment of great drama—slightly spoilt, however, by someone who chose that exact moment to crawl into the glade from the opposite direction.

Who? Our Pong, of course—and a sorry sight she looked too. There were twigs in her hair and

rips in her blouse. The hem of her red gypsy skirt had come undone and trailed in the mud. She had lost both earrings, her scarf, her shawl, both castanets and twenty-three bangles. One of her boots had the sole flapping, and she was so tired she was nearly on her hands and knees. A small bedraggled Hamster limped at her side, cheek pouches sagging with exhaustion and golden fur soaked with perspiration. Both of them looked just about all in.

"I'm sorry, Sharky!" croaked Pongwiffy. "I know you'll never forgive me, but we did our best. We've been trailing it all day, but we just couldn't catch it, could we, Hugo? Badness knows where it's gone, we've looked everywhere . . ." And then she stopped, eyes on stalks as she spotted The Cake on the stretcher. There it was, all two hundred candles blazing merrily, not a crumb out of place.

"What are you babbling about, Pongwiffy?" said Sourmuddle. "You're late for my party. And why are you dressed as a scarecrow? It's not fancy dress, y'know. Now, stop trying to hog the limelight. This is my night, and I'm going to enjoy it. Just let me feast my eyes for one moment on That Cake. My, that's Some Cake, that is."

"This is my cousin, Pierre de Gingerbeard, Sourmuddle. You know, the famous chef? He made it especially for you," said Sharkadder.

"Well, I'm very honored, I'm sure," said Sourmuddle, and Pierre de Gingerbeard gave a stiff little bow and said the honor was his.

"Blow out the candles," urged the Witches when the cake was transferred from the stretcher to the center of the trestle table. Wiping away a tear, Sourmuddle blew out the candles as the Witches sang ten more choruses of *Happy Birthday* and six of *For She's a Jolly Good Fellow*. It took that long because you don't have much puff when you're two hundred.

"Hooray!" everyone cheered as the last candle flickered out. "Cut it now, Sourmuddle!"

Sourmuddle took a sharp knife and solemnly cut the first slice.

"I now declare this tea open!" she bellowed, taking a vast bit—and with happy cries, the Witches fell upon the trestle tables and began to stuff themselves in earnest.

"Come on, Pong," said Sharkadder kindly, going up and putting her arm around her drooping friend. "Come and eat something before you fall down."

"I don't understand," muttered Pongwiffy weakly. "Is that the same Cake?"

"Of course. Let's go and grab a slice before it's all gone."

"But how? Why? We've been searching for it all day, but the Rolling Spell made it go too fast, you see, and we just couldn't catch up . . ."

"Rolling spell? What, you used another of those wonky old spells of yours? That explains it."

"Explains what?"

"Well, you see, after I came around from my faint, I flew straight to the Gingerbeard Kitchens to see if Cousin Pierre had a spare sponge or something, and we were just talking about what an idiot you were when in it rolled, just like that. A bit battered, of course, but Cousin Pierre soon repaired the damage. I suppose it's a homing cake. Like homing pigeons, you know. I'm surprised you didn't think of that. It's obvious it'd make for home. Why, what are you doing, Pong?"

"Crying," said Pongwiffy, who was.

"Well, don't. Not at a party. Everything turned out all right in the end, didn't it? No bones broken."

"You haven't seen my knees. I fell over at least a million times, and Hugo got stuck down a rabbit hole, and then there was the bull . . ."

"Yes, well, tell me all about it when you get your strength back. Come on, Pong, it's a party. You love parties." And firmly, she led Pongwiffy toward the trestle tables.

After a cup of bogwater, Pongwiffy felt a little better. After seventeen sausage rolls and four plates of trifle, she really began to perk up. By her sixth dish of ice cream, she felt ready to join in the games, and by her ninth chocolate éclair, there was no holding her back.

But if Pongwiffy enjoyed herself, you should have seen Sourmuddle. Two hundred years old she might have been, but you'd never have known it. She danced jig after jig with Pierre de Gingerbeard until he finally begged to be allowed to collapse on the spot. Then she danced a few on her own, only sitting down when Agglebag and Bagaggle's violins became so hot they couldn't play them anymore.

She joined in all the party games and, owing to her incredible energy and remarkable talent for cheating, won every prize. Nobody complained, because after all, it was her birthday. Besides, everyone was busily being smarmy in the hopes that they might be chosen as Grandwitch. So they smiled when Sourmuddle tripped them up and pushed them off the chairs in Musical Chairs, laughed when she blew squeakers in their faces, joined loudly in the songs about how great she was and didn't even complain when, in an excess

of high spirits, she poured trifle down the back of their robes. What a time Sourmuddle had!

She was still going strong when dawn broke, and had to be forcibly strapped on to the cake stretcher and carried home, still giggling, and startling the early birds with vigorous blasts of song.

Pongwiffy, Hugo, Dudley and Sharkadder went with her, to help Snoop get her safely tucked up in bed. They tipped the Dwarfs who carried the stretcher with Pongwiffy's Magic Coin—the one which always returns to her purse ten minutes later. That was mean, but Witches are like that. The Dwarfs tipped their caps and trudged off back to

Crag Hill again, where their master lay snoring with his head on the silver platter of cake crumbs. It took them the whole of that day to cart him back up the Misty Mountain. They were the only ones who didn't enjoy the party.

It took ages to get Sourmuddle undressed and into bed, because of the alarming amount of weapons and Magical bits and pieces they found all over her—but finally it was done. Hugo and Dudley placed all her presents on her bedside table, so that she could look at them whilst she went to sleep.

"I don't see one from you, Pongwiffy," Sourmuddle remarked, yawning.

"I haven't given it to you yet," explained Pongwiffy, thinking of the gift-wrapped dustbin she had spent the last week scraping out. "I had other things on my mind."

"Pong helped me organize the Cake, you know," said Sharkadder loyally. "She's worked very hard to make your birthday a success."

"To be sure. You all have. I never had a better time in my life."

"I—er—I suppose you'll be thinking of retiring now," said Pongwiffy. "Now you're two hundred."

"Who, me? Retire? Not on your life. Not till I'm four hundred. I've always said that. You'd better start thinking about planning my retirement party soon, you know. There's only another two hundred years to go. Good-night."

And with that, she blew out her bedside candle and began to snore.

There was a silence. Then:

"Oh well," said Sharkadder with a sigh. "Might as well go home, I suppose. I don't expect she wanted to say it in front of you."

"Say what?" said Pongwiffy, following her out.

"Well, it's obvious she was joking. Of course she plans to retire. I expect she'll tell me in the morning."

"Tell you what? *What?*"

"That I'm to be Grandwitch, of course. I mean, I'm the obvious choice."

"Quite right," growled Dudley.

"Obvious choice? YOU?" howled Pongwiffy. "Hear that, Hugo? Talk about stuck-up. If anyone's going to be chosen, it'll be me. Who's got the toughest familiar? Eh? Eh?"

"True," chipped in Hugo.

"What's true?" snarled Dudley. "If it weren't fer me bad back . . ."

"And who organized the talent contest?" howled Pongwiffy. "And who got the cake from the Goblins? Me, that's who."

"Don't be ridiculous," sneered Sharkadder. "You need somebody with good dress sense representing the Coven. Not some smelly old tramp in a torn cardigan."

"Smelly old tramp . . . are you referring to me? D'you know the first thing I'll do when I'm Grandwitch? I'll break friends with you, and have you thrown out of the Coven!" raged Pongwiffy.

"Oh ha ha ha!" jeered Sharkadder, flouncing

along. "Come on Dudley. I don't want you associating with that Hamster. It's been badly brought up. When your back's better, you can teach it who's boss."

" 'E can teach me now if 'e like," snapped Hugo challengingly. "Come on, vindbag. Vant a fight?"

"Oh, me back, me back . . ."

"Thrown out of the Coven! Thrown out of the Coven!" taunted Pongwiffy.

"Stinkpot. You stink, Pongwiffy, admit it. 'Scuse me while I put this clothes peg on my nose . . ."

And so the arguments raged on and the insults flew as they all strolled home through the early morning dew.

About the Author

KAYE UMANSKY was born in Plymouth in Devon, England. She went to Teacher's Training College, after which she taught in London primary schools for twelve years, specializing in music and drama. In her spare time, she sang and played keyboards with a semiprofessional soul band.

She now writes full time and has written more than twenty-five books of fantasy, fiction, and poetry for children. She draws on traditional folktales and modern urban myths for her inspiration and has a sense of humor that is popular with children of all ages, from five to one hundred and five. She lives in London with her family.

Among her most popular books are her hilarious Pongwiffy titles. *Pongwiffy, Pongwiffy and the Goblins' Revenge,* and *Pongwiffy and the Spell of the Year,* which won the Nottinghamshire Book Award, are available from Minstrel Books.